The Finding Place

The Finding Place

Julie Hartley

Red Deer Press

Published in Canada by Red Deer Press, 195 Allstate Parkway, Markham, Ontario L3R 4T8
Published in the United States by Red Deer Press, 311 Washington Street, Brighton, Massachusetts 02135

www.reddeerpress.com

10 9 8 7 6 5 4 3 2 1

Red Deer Press acknowledges with thanks the Canada Council for the Arts, and the Ontario Arts Council for their support of our publishing program. We acknowledge the financial support of the Government of Canada through the Canada Book Fund (CBF) for our publishing activities.

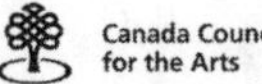

We acknowledge the financial support of the Government of Canada
Nous reconnaissons l'appui financier du gouvernement du Canada
Canada

Library and Archives Canada Cataloguing in Publication
Hartley, Julie, author
Finding place/ Julie Hartley.
ISBN 978-0-88995-533-2
Data available on file.

Publisher Cataloging-in-Publication Data (U.S.)
Hartley, Julie, author
Finding place/ Julie Hartley.
ISBN 978-0-88995-533-2
Data available on file.

Edited for the Press by Peter Carver
Cover and text design by Daniel Choi
Printed in Canada by Friesens Corporation

for Craig

and for our wonderful daughter

The End

On our last holiday as a family, the sun just shone and shone.

It was March Break and we were staying in Mexico, in a jungle town where all the buildings were yellow. Houses, shops, everything. All a glorious sunshine yellow.

Carriages rumbled along the cobbled streets, pulled by horses with flowers in their manes. One of them stopped for us. Dad lifted Mom and me onto the cushioned seat and jumped up beside us, singing his nonsense English songs the entire time. The driver started to sing loudly in Spanish to drown out Dad's song. Dad sang even louder, then the two of them looked at each other and laughed. Their laughter echoed on and on like it was never going to end.

Our ride finished in front of a monastery that had yellow walls and beautiful arches with vivid yellow crosses on the top. Dad leapt to the ground. He handed Mom down as if she were a queen, then swung me through the air like I was a little kid again. He took my hand and ran with me across the road, to buy me a mango on a stick. Someone had carved the fruit to look like petals on a rose.

Later we climbed a pyramid together, struggling upward through the heat. The pyramid was crumbling and very old. It stood in the center of town, with the yellow monastery behind and jungle stretching in all directions. Jeweled lizards stared up at us from the warm stones as we climbed.

There was a boy at the top of the pyramid, all alone. He was maybe eight or nine years old and he was flying a kite. A homemade one: plastic garbage bags at the end of a length of twine. The kite was riding a current, way up above the pyramid, over the rainforest and the magical yellow town. He looked so sure of himself, that boy, staring upward with a wide smile on his face, as if it wasn't a plastic-bag kite at the end of his string but the whole world.

Maybe that's why I asked The Question again, right then. Because that boy seemed like the opposite of me.

"Who were my birth parents, Dad? Sometimes I feel like I don't know who I am."

He could have repeated what they usually said every time I asked. That I had been found when I was one day old outside a village school somewhere in Guangxi, China. Left there, probably, because I was a girl and my birth parents needed a son to help them in the fields. He could have told me again that I'd only had an orphanage to call home for the first few months of my life, until he and Mom came to adopt me.

But that day, up on top of the pyramid, Dad said something different. Something I won't ever forget.

"Look at this boy flying his kite," he whispered, leaning close. "What do you see? A regular Mexican kid who lives in a yellow town built by the Spaniards. But look again."

We all looked in silence at the boy, his head turned to the sky.

"He isn't just Mexican, this child. He's Mayan as well. His

ancestors built an empire. Cities in the jungle and pyramids like the one we're standing on. They were artists, warriors, thinkers. Does he know any of this in a way he could explain? Maybe not. But it's still a part of him, deep inside."

The sun beat down on our heads and everything shimmered.

"Kelly, it's the same with you. You are Chinese in the way this boy is Mayan. It's inside of you and always will be. Each of us is filled with mysteries we cannot begin to understand."

Dad made me feel so important that day. No longer lost because I didn't know where I came from, but strong because there was so much inside of me, waiting to be discovered. And just as this boy had his regular life as a Mexican kid, so I had my Canadian life with Mom and Dad.

When I think of our family, I often think about that afternoon on top of the pyramid. The three of us holding hands. Those lizards gazing at us from the stones. And the small boy who seemed so big, reaching up above the jungle and the town, holding the world on the end of a string.

Part 1

CANADA

1
Mom

It was exactly one year later when the men came to take away Dad's swords.

Snow was falling in thick flakes as I trudged home, trailing my backpack along the ground. I turned the corner and there they were, outside our house. Two men, each with bushy beards and large hands. They had already loaded most of Dad's stuff into crates marked *Broadswords: Handle With Care.* The crates were stacked on the sidewalk. As I watched, they lifted the top one, carried it to their van, and slid it into the back like a coffin. A cloud passed in front of the sun and the street began to darken. It felt as if night had come too soon.

I began to run, skidding across the road, around their van, up our front path, and in through the open door.

All down our hallway the walls were bare. Thin strips of unfaded wallpaper showed the places where the swords used to hang. Only Dad's mace and cutlass were left, propped against the door frame. And there was one more crate left in the hallway. On the side it said: *Fragile—Rapiers.*

Where was Mom? Why was she letting this happen?

Then I heard laughter coming from the kitchen. All this stuff going on—Dad being torn a little more out of our lives—and Mom was laughing like everything was okay.

"What's going on?"

She was pacing around the kitchen, the phone balanced on her shoulder and a Snickers bar in her hand. When she saw me, her smile fell away. She stopped moving, the candy bar halfway to her mouth.

"I said, what's going on!" I dropped my backpack and coat on the floor and kicked off my winter boots.

"Hold on a minute, Lou," Mom said into the phone. Then she put her hand over the receiver.

"You're home early," she said.

"I guess you weren't expecting that." I glanced over my shoulder. The men were returning for the last crate. Dad's rapiers.

"How come you're home so early?" Mom's voice was high pitched, like she was on the edge of laughter, or tears.

"Mandarin class was canceled," I said. "Did you think you'd have this done before I got home?"

"Kelly, I never liked them, you know that. Swords are more than just stage combat props. They're weapons. I don't want them in the house."

"You haven't got the right."

"I have no choice."

"This stuff is Dad's!"

Mom took a step toward me and I moved back. When she spoke again, her voice was more under control.

"Sweetie, if your dad had wanted the swords, he would have taken them with him."

"It's only been a few weeks! What if he wants them when he moves back?"

"I don't think he—"

"Don't say it." A sob rose in my throat and I swallowed it, just in time. "What if Dad gets a film job and he needs the swords?" I said. "What about Sherwood Productions? What if they have sword fights in their next show?"

"Kelly, we've had this discussion. Sherwood was your Dad's theater company. With him gone, it doesn't exist anymore."

A voice boomed in the hallway behind me, loud enough to make both of us jump.

"These going too, are they?"

It was one of the delivery men. He must have been from the North of England because he had an accent just like Dad's. He was holding the mace in one hand and the cutlass in the other.

"Be careful with those!" I shouted. He moved forward; his body and the two weapons filled the doorway.

"Yes, those can go," Mom told him. "That's the last of them."

The man looked from Mom to me and back again. When someone does that, you know what's coming even before they open their mouth.

"This your daughter?" he asked Mom in what she always

called an Outdoor Voice. The man's right glove was off. His fingers were thick and hairy, not like Dad's at all. I didn't want him in our house.

"Yes," Mom said, sounding tired all of a sudden. "This is my daughter." I glared at her. Why did she think she always had to answer their questions? Just because we looked different from each other, that didn't make our relationship everyone's business.

"She's tall," the man said. I knew what he really meant because people said it all the time. *She's tall for a Chinese person.* Dad and I used to laugh at the dumb things people said sometimes, but it was hard to remember what we'd ever found funny, now he was gone.

"Asian people come in more than one size, you know," I said.

"Kelly—" Mom's voice carried a warning.

"And anyway, I'm not Chinese. I'm probably more Canadian than you."

The man wasn't listening. He swung the mace up and over his shoulder, narrowly missing the wood trim around the door. Then he carried on as if I hadn't said a thing. "My neighbor's sister, she adopted three kids," he said to Mom. "China, I think they were from. Little one's only six. Cute as a button. Bright, too. They're all bright."

I wasn't sure if he meant all three kids, or all Chinese people. Either way, I'd had enough.

"You can go now."

"Kelly!"

The man looked suddenly uncomfortable. "Right you are,

then," he said. A phrase Dad used a lot. He reached past me and handed Mom an envelope, then he turned and left. The front door banged shut behind him and the noise echoed down the empty hall.

"You were rude," Mom said.

I stared straight at her—confrontational, Dad would have called it—and made my voice calm, because it would sound more menacing that way. "If it only takes a few weeks for you to sell Dad's stuff," I said, "then how much longer before you find yourself a new boyfriend?"

Mom looked mad. Judging by the expression she had on her face, you wouldn't even think she loved me anymore. "I'll pretend you didn't say that," she said, her voice as low and calm as mine. She lifted her hand off the phone and raised it to her ear. She was going to continue her chat with Auntie Lou as if nothing had happened.

That's when I kind of lost it.

"How long, Mom? Three more weeks? Six, maybe?" I was yelling now. "Will someone else be living here when Dad gets back?"

Mom slammed the phone down on the kitchen counter.

"Kelly—I've had enough. You're thirteen now and that's old enough to show some self-control. Go to your room. I mean it. Right now."

I grabbed my backpack, stomping up the stairs and into my room. Then I slammed the door behind me.

What I needed more than anything was to call Raizel. I emptied the backpack upside down on my bed and rummaged through it, looking for the phone. Mom's phone. The one I wasn't technically supposed to have, though Mom didn't use it, and mostly it lived inside my bag. But there was too much school stuff, too many Mandarin books, everything getting in the way. And I was too mad to focus properly. I whipped the door open again and yelled, "I'm quitting Mandarin, in case you're interested!" Mom needed to see she wasn't the only one who could wipe things out of our lives.

There was only silence from downstairs.

I took a deep breath and yelled again.

"How come we're not even taking a trip for March Break, eh? Is our whole life over because Dad's gone away for a bit?"

No answer.

Slamming the door again, I turned back to the heap of stuff on my bed. Books, papers, pens, snack wrappers, and, in the middle of it all, Mom's phone. When I turned it on, though, the screen glowed green then faded straight to black. Dead battery.

No Raizel, then.

I sat down on the bed.

"You'll be all reight, flower," Dad would have said, sliding a big hand across my shoulder. He always made his accent stronger if he was trying to cheer me up. "Chin up, lass." Then a playful shove. Tickles. Laughter. And a cuddle. Even remembering it made me feel better. You couldn't stay in a mood for long around Dad.

"I *know* those swords were important to you, Dad," I told

him, still trying to feel the weight of his hand on my back. "They were important to both of us. And now they're gone. Another piece of you gone. Soon there won't be anything left."

I breathed deeply and counted to a hundred. Gradually, my hands stopped shaking.

I looked up. This was my room, and at least no one could take that from me. The row of stuffed pandas on my pillow. The duvet with hundreds of birds on it that Dad bought for me when I was small. And the photos hanging on my closet door. One of the photos had a pretty silver frame. It was a picture of me at just ten months old and was taken in China, on the day we became a family. I was wearing a funny embroidered jacket, padded to make me look fatter than I really was, and my dark hair stood up on end. It's hard to believe this strange-looking baby is a part of who I am. That photo had been hanging on my closet door for as long as I could remember, but recently I'd taped another underneath. A photo of Mom and Dad taken last year in Mexico. In it, they have their arms wrapped tightly round each other and they are smiling.

Both these photos made me uncomfortable now. The baby photo made me feel kind of lost, like I couldn't recognize myself, and the one of Mom and Dad was a big lie because they didn't love each other, and that meant they probably never had, not really. I peeled it off the door and tore it down the middle. Then I stuck one piece on each side of my baby photo. But that wasn't right, either. In real life, Dad wasn't beside me anymore. I took him down and, as I did, the Mom part of the photo slid to the floor. That left the little framed photo all alone on the closet door, and suddenly it seemed like the saddest thing ever. The very Chinese baby with the funny clothes and the wide startled eyes, totally alone without anyone to love her. Me.

I opened the bedroom door and listened. Silence. Mom wasn't talking on the phone. There wasn't even the sound of a radio, or the clattering noise she always made as she emptied the dishwasher. Had Mom left now, too? I crept out and peered over the banister. Nothing. So I moved slowly down the stairs.

Mom had made herself a cup of tea. She was sipping it at the kitchen table, a pile of papers in front of her and a bottle of Tylenol in her hand. She looked up when I came in, but she didn't tell me to go back to my room. Instead she said, "Kelly, we need to talk. I need to tell you some things."

I moved a bit closer. Not much. Just a few steps.

"Why did you sell Dad's swords?" I asked. My voice wasn't angry anymore. I just felt relieved that she was still there. "Why did Dad go? Where is he?"

"I wish I could give you those answers," Mom said, "but I can't." Her eyes closed slowly then opened again. "I know how hard this is. For you and for me. But we do need to chat."

"Why can't I phone him? Why don't we even know his number?"

"Try to listen for one moment. Please."

Mom tipped three pills into her palm, tossed her head back, and swallowed them all at once. When she leaned forward, loose curls unraveled over her eyes. Mom has always taken pride in her appearance, especially her hair, constantly altering it to make herself look younger than she really is. Only now her hair didn't look lovely at all. Just unwashed and uncared for.

She didn't speak straightaway and, when she did, it seemed like she'd changed the subject completely.

"Do you still wonder about the past?" she asked. "Maybe about where you came from? Where you were born?"

"What does that have to do with anything?"

"Just answer me. Do you still wonder about who you are?"

"I know who I am."

"I mean, who you were when you were a baby. What happened before we became a family?"

"Nope," I lied.

"Kelly, you used to ask questions all the time about being adopted. Now you never do. You keep everything bottled up inside. That isn't healthy."

"I said no."

"It's just that you're not yourself anymore."

I turned away from her and pulled a Coke from the fridge.

"I don't care about the China stuff, Mom," I told her. "All I care about is why you and Dad started fighting and why he went away."

I left a lot unspoken behind those words and she knew it. Mom was the real problem. If it wasn't for her, if she hadn't nagged at Dad all the time and tried to turn him into something he wasn't, then maybe he would still be here.

"Kelly, please sit down. Like I said, we have to talk."

I reached for a chair, and I meant to sit and listen—really I did. Maybe if I had, we would have actually started to communicate, like two human beings who still cared about each other. Maybe Mom would have shared things, answered my questions, and everything could have been different. But instead, as I leaned forward, I saw something on the table. It was a check. The one left by the men who took the swords. I picked it up and looked at it closely. A check for five thousand dollars. Then I let go. It drifted back down to the table.

"That's Dad's money," I said.

"Kelly, it isn't—"

"That money is Dad's. He saved up for every one of those swords. It took him years and years to collect them all. You know it did. That's Dad's money."

Mom's eyes met mine. "And while he was spending money on his toys, all those years, who do you think paid the bills?" she said. "Who do you think pays them now?"

I grabbed my coat off the floor. I was trembling so much I could hardly get my arms in it.

"I don't care. It's still stealing."

"You're being ridiculous."

"It is, Mom. You're stealing from Dad. You always tell me to do the right thing. That money belongs to Dad. It's not yours."

"Kelly, calm down. When you get angry, you say and do things—"

"You know what I think?" I stopped struggling with my coat and looked at her. "I think we should wait until Dad tells us where he is, then I'll take the check to him myself.

And maybe I'll stay. Because I want to be with my dad."

This was something I'd been dreaming of for weeks, but it still felt terrible, like a betrayal, speaking the thought out loud. There was a part of me that wanted to take the words back as soon as I said them. But it also felt good to finally get this out in the open.

Mom said nothing. She had two fingers of each hand pressed hard against her temples.

I moved into the hallway and pulled on my boots, leaning back against the bare wall where the swords used to hang.

"I'm going out," I shouted. "To the library, then to Raizel's. I'll make my own way home."

Mom slid her head into her hands, using the tips of her fingers to massage both her temples. That's why it was a struggle to hear what she was saying. Because she was speaking down into the table.

"If you keep on talking to me like this, Kelly, there are going to be consequences."

For Mom, actions always had consequences. For Dad, consequences never existed.

"I'm off."

Mom lifted her head slowly, as if it weighed too much. But she didn't turn to look at me. Her eyes stayed closed.

"We have to talk, Kelly. Please. There's something important I have to tell you. Something we need to discuss."

But I didn't stay. I was too choked up, too upset. Instead, I clomped upstairs in my snow boots and shoveled all the stuff back into my bag. Then I ran down the stairs and out the front door, slamming it hard behind me.

2
Dad

When I reached the library, I walked straight past and kept on going. I still felt pretty upset and, when I'm emotional, things don't go as planned. I just follow my feelings.

Like Mom said, Sherwood Productions had closed down when Dad went away. The studio had been locked and deserted for weeks now and I hadn't been back there, not even once. Now, it was the one place I could think of where maybe nothing had changed. If no one had been in yet to clear it out, then it was going to feel as if time had stopped on the day Dad left. As if the past few weeks hadn't happened at all.

It was getting dark now. Snow was still falling, and an icy wind slashed the air like one of Dad's swords. An occasional car passed by, moving in slow motion, but the sidewalks were deserted except for me. I turned onto Roncesvalles Avenue, then ducked down an alley like we always used to. Dad's special shortcut. He spoke about it like a secret he shared only with me. There was a line of garages on both sides, all of them spray-painted with colorful graffiti. My favorite was the open mouth screaming. It reached the whole length of the garage door and continued up onto the roof. By day it was pretty cool. In the dark, though, when you were all by yourself, it was scary. Terrifying, even.

I reached the end of the alley, climbed through a hole in the fence, and there I was, at the back of the Art Factory. Looming above me was a red brick wall, almost every window in it either cracked or smashed. A rusted metal stairway began on the left hand side of the wall and zigzagged up to the top. I jumped over the bottom step as usual—the metal was bent upward, twisted and dangerous—then started to climb.

Many of the studios were dark. They'd been abandoned long ago, and now they held nothing but garbage and broken furniture. Dad said that one day the City would evict everyone, tear the building down, and then developers would come and put up a trendy condo instead. But it hadn't happened yet. A weak light shone through a grimy third floor window and, as I climbed past, I saw a woman in a long white shirt, standing in front of an enormous canvas splattered with yellow paint. On the fifth floor, there were other signs of life: musical instruments, rows of mirrors, dance barres.

The stairway was rickety up at the top, the railings slippery with ice and snow. It ended with a narrow platform just under the roof, and a door made of gray metal with a sign painted in uneven letters: *Sherwood Productions*. The sign was familiar, but the notice taped underneath it wasn't. It was written in now-faded red marker and fastened to the gray paint with clear duct tape. It said: *Rehearsals Postponed until Further Notice.*

The handwriting was my dad's.

I looked closer and that's when I saw it.

At the bottom of the notice was another sentence: *In Case of Emergency Please Contact ...*

I ripped the paper off the door, my heart thumping with excitement, and held it up to my eyes. The ink had run, and there were spots of mold between the letters. Even so, I could still make out Dad's name. And below it, an address.

I felt so triumphant in that moment that I wanted to slide all the way down to the ground and run out onto the road, screaming to the world that I knew where to find my dad.

Then I read the address again, and excitement turned into confusion.

Vancouver. The address on the posting was for Vancouver. That was thousands of miles away.

Why would my dad go so far away? And why Vancouver? He didn't have any friends there, at least not that I knew of. He'd never talked about going out west. And everything he'd always loved was right here in Toronto: his home, his theater company, and me. It didn't make any sense.

Maybe Dad was leaving a false trail. Tricking anyone who came here, so they would think he was far away, when really he wasn't. But why would he do that?

Was my dad in some kind of trouble?

Mom always says I have an overactive imagination ... but what if?

I felt around on top of the doorframe for the key. For seconds I held my breath, worried that maybe Dad might have taken it with him. My fingers swept across icy metal, then closed around something long and thin. I turned the key in the lock and went inside.

The smell hit me first, and I was filled with memories so overpowering that, for a moment, I couldn't move. It was a smell I knew from so many days spent here with Dad, over years and years. A smell I'd missed so much over the last few weeks. Dust. Old clothes. Perfume and makeup. Mothballs. Greasepaint and dreams. The scent of actors and excitement. The scent of my dad. I stood there for a long time in the dark, shivering as I breathed it all in. Then I hit the light switch.

The rehearsal room had always been lit by a single bulb, swaying from a cord in the middle of the ceiling. That was enough in the daytime, with several long windows on each side to let in sunshine, but in the dark it was creepy. Everything around the walls shivered in shadow. I walked into the middle of the studio and my feet clop-clopped on the wooden planks. I'd never been here alone before. I'd always been with Dad and the others. Now, a space that normally boomed with loud voices, laughter, and music, was dead quiet and freezing cold.

Colorful masks, shields, and helmets hung untidily from nails along the walls. There were rows and rows of costumes at the back, disappearing into darkness. In the corners, stage flats were propped one against the other. There was a miniature turret behind the door. A throne, studded with plastic jewels. Even a dragon's head taller than me, hanging from the ceiling. I'd helped make so many of these sets and props. This magic had been my world for almost my entire life. Now, it felt as if I were moving like a ghost through it all. As if a decade had passed, not just weeks, and no one else was left alive. I touched costumes, tried on wigs, held a jeweled goblet in my hand.

Then I reached the Director's Table.

It was a trestle table, painted sky blue, with dozens of names and messages scratched into the surface. Dad liked to sit behind it when he was directing, while the actors ran their scenes. Sometimes, he'd let me sit beside him. As always, the table was stacked with yellowing scripts from productions that went back to before I was born, but there was something new there, as well. Right in the middle of the table. A black jewelry box. I picked it up and opened the lid.

Inside was my dad's wedding ring.

And that's when I heard the noise.

It could have been a mouse, maybe. Or even the sound of snow falling from the roof. Either way, I felt sure, all of a sudden, that I wasn't alone. The bare light bulb was swaying and the shadows on the walls and across the floor shivered. I turned toward the long rows of costumes, squinting into the dark.

That's when I saw him.

"Dad? Daddy?"

It was unmistakable. It was him.

He stood in shadow between two racks of velvet gowns. I couldn't see his face but I could see the shape of him. The brocade jacket with its shiny green buttons that he had worn in so many shows.

I wanted to rush into his arms, to bury my head in his coat and sob because I'd been so alone, but now he was back. I wanted to cry out all the sadness of the past few weeks, then ask him why he had left me, and listen as he said how sorry he was. But I couldn't do it. Something held me back. We'd been apart for such a long time that the distance between us wouldn't close. Crossing the floor of the studio and hugging my dad was suddenly the hardest thing in the world to do.

I walked toward him slowly.

"Dad? Is that you? It's okay, Dad. There's no one else here. It's just me. Kelly."

Was something wrong with him? Why didn't he move? Wasn't he pleased to see me?

"I missed you, Dad. Did you miss me? Why did you go away?"

I was almost touching the figure before I realized it didn't have a face. Only hair bigger and blacker than Dad's and, below the hair, just emptiness where the face should have been. And a thick metal rod, passing from the hair to the brocade jacket that still held my dad's unique smell. There were no hands, either. Just empty air at the end of the sleeves where Dad's hands should have been.

A mannequin. Dad's theater jacket. His pants and knee-high boots. His smell.

My dad, but not my dad at all.

And now the rehearsal space felt like a tomb. Not just silent and dark, but full of dead things. When I thought of everything that had happened here, I didn't feel happiness anymore. The memories filled me with sadness and grief.

I turned back to the Director's Table and scooped up the little box containing Dad's wedding ring. Then I stuffed the notice with Dad's address into my pocket and left the building as quickly as possible, half running, half tumbling down the stairs of the fire escape, past the abandoned studios, the cracked and smashed windows, the artist splattering a canvas with sunshine yellow paint, all the way to the ground. Along the alley and back to Roncesvalles where there were lights and cars and some of the shops were still open. I didn't look behind me even once.

I'd never go back there again. Sherwood Productions was closed and, with it, a part of me was gone for good.

I liked being in the library after dark. The homework room felt cozy and safe, all the little desk lamps with their orange light, and darkness pooling, soft and warm, in the corners. The world rushed on by outside the windows, but inside, everything stood still.

I sat for a long time at one of the terminals, not even thinking, just trying to get calm and in control again. Gulping down tears until they stopped. Then I started to write.

To: director@sherwoodprod.com
Subject: Please Don't Forget Me

Dear Dad,
I've written to you so many times now, without a single reply. Maybe you don't check this account very often, now you're not running Sherwood. Or maybe you're suffering with some personal stuff and you need your space. Weeks and weeks of it. When Raizel's aunt got depression, she didn't want to speak to anyone for over a month. So maybe it's something like that. And if it is, then, when you're ready, I want you to open your email and find all these messages. That way, you'll know I still love you and, when the time is right, maybe you'll come back.

Our lives are falling apart now you're not here. Mom and I argue all the time, and I also have to put up with Auntie Lou. Remember how you'd make jokes about "Loopy Lou" behind her back? She must have known you didn't like her very much. Now, with you gone, she's nosing her way into our lives. Mom spends ages on the phone with her most nights, probably complaining about me. The two of them have secrets, Dad, and they shut me out of everything, like I'm just a little kid. You never treated me like that.

Mom's so different these days. She's even stopped painting because she says it makes her headaches worse, and you know how grumpy she gets when she doesn't paint. I've stopped a bunch of stuff, too, even the Tai Chi. That belonged to the two of us together, and I don't want to do it by myself.

Remember the kite last year in Mexico? How you held on to Mom on top of that pyramid, like you still loved her? We laughed so much that day.

Why didn't you tell us you were going to Vancouver? Or maybe you're not in Vancouver at all. I don't know what to believe.

Please come back, Dad. I miss you.

Kelly

Writing to Dad made me feel a bit better and, afterward, I sat at the computer in the peaceful silence of the homework room, just thinking. Then I did something I probably shouldn't have done. I opened Mom's gmail account.

I'd thought about doing this many times over the past weeks. Mom's behavior was a mystery to me and I needed to know what she was thinking. What was going on inside her head. But spying on people is not cool. You have to be pretty desperate. And now I was.

It wasn't hard to figure out Mom's password because she uses the same one for everything she does online—my Chinese name, the one given to me by the orphanage when I was just a day old. I typed it in and a long list of emails appeared. The most recent was to Auntie Lou, sent less than an hour ago. It was strange to think of Mom sitting in the kitchen, writing her side of everything, while I was sitting in the library writing mine. And neither one of us sharing with the other.

What I read in the email came as a total shock.

To: lynt@bolsover.ca
Subject: Kelly

Lou,
I tried to talk with Kelly again tonight and, as usual, it didn't go well. She was furious about the swords. How can I explain why we need the money?

Yes, I know. I've left it too late. I should have told her days ago.

It's easy to make sense of this to myself and to you. But to Kelly? How can I say it? "Sweetheart, you've lost a lot in your life. Not only your dad, but your birth parents and birth culture. I can't bring your dad back, but I can help you make sense of those other losses. And that might help both of us to move forward."

Can you see how ridiculous this will sound to her? If she even bothers to listen. First mention of her dad and she flies off the handle. Disappears out the door. And I know what you're thinking. Time is running out.

The tickets arrived this afternoon. Toronto to Beijing, return. We fly there direct and through Vancouver on the way back. My plan is to be ready when Kelly gets home tonight. That's when I'll tell her that we leave for China on Sunday.

3

Raizel

"Raizel! I have to talk to you, right now!"

I flung open the door to Café Chocolat and practically fell inside.

It was busier than usual. There was so much chatter and laughter that no one even turned to look when the door slammed behind me. The air was steamy as warm milk and smelled like chocolate syrup.

Raizel's mom was behind the counter. She was wearing her usual funky clothes: a long skirt with big orange flowers on it, a sparkly scarf, and a fedora instead of a hairnet. Cara's so young and pretty that you'd think she was Raizel's big sister rather than her mom. That's because she was only nineteen when Raizel was born. My mom is practically decades older. Old enough to be my granny, maybe.

"Cara!" I shouted. "Is Raizel around?"

She pointed to the corner table. "Fraternizing with the customers, as usual. Be a darling—take this to table five, would you?"

Raizel's mom handed me a little silver tray with a slip of paper on it. Beside the bill were two handmade strawberry chocolates. They used to be my favorite when I was little but, now that I'm older, I prefer the cappuccino creams.

I delivered the bill, then headed over to Raizel. She was wearing flared jeans with embroidered flowers on the legs, and a ton of her mom's sparkly costume jewelry. Sharing her table was an old lady who looked Asian like me.

"Kelly!" Raizel shouted when she saw me. "We were hoping you'd show up! Come meet my new friend—Miss Wu. She likes the coffee creams best, same as you!"

I gave Miss Wu the tiniest smile, then turned to Raizel.

"Can we go up to your room? I need to talk to you, like, right now."

Raizel ignored me. She pushed the empty chair toward me with her foot. "Miss Wu, Kelly's the friend I was telling you about. She comes over most nights because we're working on a graphic novel together. She's from China as well!"

I could feel my cheeks burning.

"Are you, dear?" asked the old lady. She leaned forward as if to get a better look. "*Ni hui shuo Zhongguo hua ma*?"

She was asking me if I spoke Chinese.

"A bit," I said in an almost-whisper.

"Where are you from in China, dear?"

I glanced over Raizel's shoulder to the back of the cafe, where a door marked *Private* led through to the part of the shop where she lived with her mom. I hoped she would get the hint but she didn't. "I was born near a place called Yangshuo," I told Miss Wu, without even looking at her. "But

I'm not Chinese. I'm Canadian. I've lived in Toronto almost my whole life."

"It's very beautiful around Yangshuo," Miss Wu said. Her accent only had a hint of Chinese in it. Mostly it was Canadian, like mine.

"I need to talk to you," I said again to Raizel. "In private."

"Kelly and I have been friends for, like, forever," Raizel chattered on to Miss Wu. She knocked on the wooden tabletop. It was splatter-painted every color you could think of. "See this? We did these tables before we even started kindergarten. Mom thought it would be cute. And see up there?" She pointed to the mural on the wall. A tumbling waterfall of melted chocolate. "Our moms are both painters. They painted that mural together back when we were just little kids."

Miss Wu looked up at the mural and I nudged Raizel. "Now!" I insisted.

"Okay, okay. Looks like Mom's closing up, anyway."

"Goodbye, Raizel, dear," Miss Wu said as we all stood up. She placed a hand on my shoulder. "*Zai jian*." That meant goodbye in Mandarin. But I didn't say it back. The old lady bundled up and headed out into the dark.

I ran through the door marked *Private*, up the stairs, and into Raizel's room.

"Miss Wu is really sweet," Raizel shouted, running up behind me. "You should have been nicer."

"You sound like my mom."

"I don't care. It's not cool to treat people like that."

"Well, you shouldn't tell everyone I'm Chinese. You make me feel like I don't belong."

Raizel sighed. "Okay, forget it. Catch!" One hand flew out from behind her back. She was holding a chocolate disc—the type Cara melts to make her truffles. She flicked the disc through the air. I leapt forward, my mouth open, and caught it between my teeth. It's a game we've played since we were small.

Then we smiled at each other and everything felt okay again.

Raizel's room is as funky as the chocolate shop—full of bright and sparkly fabrics that she buys with her mom from the ethnic shops in Kensington Market. We sat side by side on her bed, cross-legged, and stuffed our mouths with chocolate discs.

"So, what's up?" Raizel asked through a mouthful of chocolate.

I gulped, and a wad of gooey chocolate slid down my throat. "Mom's booked us tickets to fly to China this Sunday," I said.

"China—you're kidding! For March Break? That's totally awesome."

"No. It's not awesome, Raizel. It's really not." I spun around on the bed to look at her. "Mom just went ahead and booked it. She never even asked!"

"Right—"

"I'm the one who's from China, not her."

"Okay—"

"I don't want to go back. It's bad timing. I won't go."

"Kelly, wow ... I mean, that's extreme."

Why wasn't she getting it?

"I don't want to be in China. Not right now." I dragged Raizel's pillow onto my knee and punched my fist into it. Then I squeezed it hard, pretending it was one of my giant panda stuffies. "What if Dad comes back and I'm not even here?" Tears burned my eyes but I blinked them away.

Raizel sighed. "Kelly, do you really think, after all this time—"

"Don't say it," I snapped. "Not if you're my friend."

I pulled the scrap of paper out of my pocket, the one I'd torn off the door of Dad's studio. Raizel snatched it out of my hands.

"It says he's staying in Vancouver," I told her.

"Wow."

"Stop saying that. Dad doesn't know anyone in Vancouver. Why would he go there? I don't get it."

Raizel leapt off her bed. She rummaged around in her closet, which was a complete mess, and came back with a magnifying glass. We studied the address together.

"The ink's run pretty badly," she said, "but you can still read the whole thing."

"I know."

"Maybe he's in some kind of trouble." Raizel said. "He could be running away from something. But then, why would he leave his new address for anyone to find?"

"And why didn't he tell us first?"

"Listen." Raizel grabbed hold of my shoulders and twisted me toward her.

"What?"

"Your mom and dad argued tons before he disappeared, right?"

"Yup."

"And he knows your mom would never visit the Studio?"

"Right. She never liked going there. She said it was filthy, and she didn't get along with all of the actors."

"So what if your dad posted the address on the door, knowing only you would find it? Maybe he didn't want your mom to discover where he was—he only wanted you to find out!"

Was she right? Could the address be a secret message from Dad, just for me? But then I remembered all the unanswered emails. If Dad wanted to tell me something without Mom knowing, he only had to send an email. Unlike me, Mom didn't spy on other people's stuff.

I sprawled out on Raizel's bed, looking up at the ceiling and not speaking for a long time. Raizel slumped down beside me and waited. But she's never been much good at that.

"Do you think your mom was planning to take you to the place where you were born?" Raizel asked. "Yang—whatever?"

I felt the anger coming back a bit, which was good, because you don't cry so easily when you're angry. "I haven't a clue. And it doesn't matter because Mom can't force me to go to China. I'll ask Cara if I can stay here."

Raizel seemed unsure what to say, so she changed the subject.

"Do you want to work on our novel for a bit? Look, I did this description of Vasa." She rolled sideways, grabbed a stack of papers off the floor, and dumped them on my stomach. "Vasa should be Viking, and I think she needs to be an orphan. But in your sketches, she looks too much like Hawkgirl."

"You shouldn't work on that stuff without me," I snapped. "It's our project, not yours."

"So let's work on it."

"I don't care about it anymore, Raizel. I have more important things on my mind." I pushed the papers off my stomach and onto the bed.

We were about to argue, which would have been really bad, but at that moment, the door opened and Cara walked in.

"I need to pop to the bank, girls," she said. "The cafe's all closed up." She glanced over at me. "Kelly, dear, are you okay?"

"Sure. Never been better." I can be pretty convincing when I want.

Cara looks so different from her daughter that you'd think Raizel was adopted, like me. She has skin so pale you can see veins through it, and her hair is straight and very blonde. Raizel's skin is dusky brown. She has dark eyes and wiry black curls.

Cara blew a kiss at Raizel and left. For a while we heard movement downstairs, then the sound of the front door shutting. After that, only silence.

"There's something I don't get," Raizel said after a while.

"Where'd your mom find the cash to take you to China? I mean, you told me she was running out of money."

"She sold Dad's swords," I said. "And she's keeping all the money for herself."

"Wow."

I propped myself up on my elbows and looked at her. "Mom's taking me to China because she thinks I'm messed up," I said. "She can't bring Dad back, but she figures part of my problems come from being adopted. So she thinks that visiting China is going to make everything better."

Raizel shook her head. "Weird."

"Too right. Why didn't she ask me what I wanted? It's not China, that's for sure." I gazed up at the ceiling. There were cobwebs up there, lots of them, with hundreds of tiny flies caught inside.

"Even so," Raizel said softly, "it might be nice to see where you came from." She reached into her bedside drawer, pulled out a pink emery board, and started working on her nails. Her goal was to grow them long and make them pointy like talons, but it was taking months.

"Yesterday, a man came into the shop," Raizel said. "He knew the meaning of my name because his wife's called Raizel. Do you know what it means?" I shook my head. "It means 'Rose.' Isn't that beautiful?"

"Sure." I tried to sound interested, but my thoughts kept drifting to other things.

"My Dad gave me that name. He went away before I even got born, but he told Mom what she should call me. Then he left."

"That's kind of selfish." I bent my knees and started to balance chocolate discs on them. "Your mom should have ignored him. She had to bring you up all by herself, so why should he get to choose your name?"

Raizel said nothing.

"I hate being called Kelly," I told her.

Raizel tossed a disc in the air. It hit the ceiling, but she still caught it in her mouth on the way down.

"Why don't you use your Chinese name, then?"

"Li Xiao Mei? I can't."

"Why?"

"Because the orphanage gave it to me. They probably used the same names, over and over. It was only something to call the babies until their parents came to adopt them."

Once I'd said this out loud, it made me think. If I didn't have a real name for the first few months of my life, then who was I? I was Kelly now, but did that even mean anything? My Canadian identity came from my parents but, with Dad gone, how much of that was left?

Raizel said: "If the people who give birth to you are called your birth parents, what do they call the parents who bring you up?"

I had to think about that one.

"Dad used to say he and Mom were my 'forever family,'" I told her. "But then he goes out to buy milk and doesn't come back. No explanation. There's not much 'forever' in that, is there?" I paused. "I don't blame him, though. Mom was always trying to get him to be something he wasn't. Maybe he couldn't take it anymore."

Raizel stood up. She gathered her notes off the bed, rolled them into a tube, and slung it into her closet with all the other junk. "I never met my dad," she said. "We don't even know where he was from, though Mom thinks maybe Jamaica." She leaned hard on the closet door to make it stay shut. "People go away. They leave you. My dad. Your birth parents. Your dad. That's what they do."

I didn't get a chance to respond because, just then, we heard the sound of banging. Someone was pounding on the door to the cafe, hard.

"Your mom forgot her key?" I asked.

Raizel shook her head. "She never does. C'mon. Let's check it out."

We ran downstairs. It was dark in the cafe and the sign in the window had been turned to *Closed,* but still the knocking continued. Raizel paused, then she unfastened the latch and the door swung open. Outside, in a swirl of snow, stood Miss Wu.

"Hello again, dear. Sorry to disturb you. May I come in?"

She was speaking to Raizel, but she wasn't looking at her. She was looking past Raizel and directly at me as she stepped inside.

"I thought I still had this lying around somewhere," she said. "A little gift. For you." She smiled kindly and handed me a plastic bag. I dusted off the snow and opened it. Inside there was a book of color photographs. The front cover showed forested hills as pointy as fingers, with a muddy river snaking between them. On top of the photograph were the words: *Yangshuo: Something To Remember Her By.*

I didn't know what to say. Looking at the book made me feel sad and angry at the same time.

"Kelly?" Raizel nudged me in the ribs. I looked up at Miss Wu.

"Thank you," I said, "but I don't want it. I'm not going back to China any time soon." I held the book out to her.

Miss Wu stopped smiling. She looked hurt and, right away, I felt bad. She was an old lady and she'd struggled all the way back here, even though it was snowing hard, with a gift just for me. She was only trying to be kind.

I was going to say sorry, maybe even accept the book just to make her feel better, but that's when the phone behind the counter began to ring. Raizel glanced down at it, then up at me. "Your mom," she said.

Why was Mom calling me at Raizel's? She knew I always had her phone, so if she needed to, she could call me on that.

But perhaps she'd tried already. Mom's phone was dead.

"Hi, Mom."

"Kelly." Her voice sounded kind of flat.

"Mom, you don't have to check up—"

"Listen to me, please." Mom spoke slowly, slurring her words as if she had been drinking too much wine. "I have a migraine. A very bad one. I've called Auntie Lou. She thinks it might be best to get it checked, so she's driving me to Emergency. Make your way home. We'll be back as soon as we can."

I wondered why she didn't tell me to wait for her at Raizel's. In the past, she never liked me to be out on my own in the dark, and she didn't make me stay home all alone at night, either. Was she starting to care about me less and less every day? Then I thought of our house, and how empty and scary it would seem without either Mom or Dad waiting for me.

"Which hospital?" I asked.

"St. Joseph's. Why?"

"I'll meet you there." Saying this made me feel extremely mature. I put the phone down before she could make me promise to go straight home.

When I turned back around, both Raizel and Miss Wu were staring at me.

"It's no big deal," I said. "Mom gets these headaches sometimes, that's all. She isn't coping so well without Dad. I don't think St. Joseph's can be far from here."

Miss Wu placed a hand on my arm. "You'll need to take the streetcar south down Roncesvalles," she said. "Get your coat, dear, and I'll walk you to the nearest stop. It's on my way."

4
Lou

The snow was falling fast now. Thick, heavy flakes. The whole world sinking under the weight, so maybe it would never dig itself out.

Miss Wu could walk pretty fast for an old lady and, while I half-jogged beside her, I tried to think of how to say sorry for being so mean. I was grateful that I didn't have to be alone in the dark when I was feeling so sad and kind of abandoned but, in a way, having Miss Wu there was even harder. How could she be so nice to me? I didn't deserve it at all.

The closest streetcar stop was a couple of blocks from Raizel's place and it had a covered shelter. There was a thick layer of snow on the roof, making it feel like a cave, and through the glass and the swirling flakes, the houses and shops looked blurred, half-buried, their shapes all wrong. My neighborhood had turned into someplace strange and unfamiliar.

"I can wait here with you," Miss Wu said. "The streetcar may be a while, given this weather."

There was a long silence. We stood side by side and stared into the street. At last I said, "I'm sorry, Miss Wu."

"I know, dear." She spoke so quietly it was like a voice in my head.

I felt a weight lifting off me.

"Do you live near here?" I asked.

"Not far. After your streetcar arrives, I'll make a run for it."

The image of old Miss Wu sprinting off through the snow made me smile. Miss Wu probably got the joke, too, because she returned my smile. I stepped a little closer.

"My dad loved this kind of weather," I told her. I used the past tense, but Miss Wu didn't ask where Dad was now, like most adults would. Instead, she waited for me to go on. I tried to find words to fill the silence.

"Dad loved snowstorms, lightning, oceans, ruins—anything magical. And birds. To my dad, nothing was as magical as birds."

"He sounds like a wonderful person."

"Oh, he was. He is." I stared out into the street. There was something hypnotic about the flakes, the way they moved through the air, as if time was slowing down. "In spring, Dad always took me to the Leslie Street Spit," I said. "We'd bike to the end to watch the herons. Thousands of them, nesting in the trees. Herons sitting on eggs and herons everywhere in the sky. We'd stand still until the birds forgot about us, then we'd close our eyes and just listen. The beating of a thousand pairs of wings."

Miss Wu turned and looked at me.

"I'll never go there again," I told her. "Not without Dad."

And then she started to ask. "Your dad, dear, is he ..."

If I answered, then maybe the tears would come again, so I just kept chattering on, sort of mindlessly, instead.

"When I was little, I used to think China was magical," I told her. "Just like the picture on the front cover of your book." She probably thought this was a change of subject, but it wasn't. I gazed out onto the sidewalk. Drifts were piling up against the entrance to the shelter. Maybe they'd block us both in there, inside our white cave, forever.

"Yangshuo is beautiful," Miss Wu said.

I shook my head. "I don't mean like that. I mean really magical, like in fairy stories. Filled with emperors and dragons and things. But last winter I met this girl. Jade. At a Chinese New Year banquet put on by our adoption agency. She'd been to China for real."

I knew Miss Wu was listening, but she didn't say anything when I paused. She waited for me to go on.

"Jade said they didn't even have proper toilets where she was," I said. "Only holes in the ground."

I wanted Miss Wu to laugh because this was more ridiculous than emperors and dragons. But she didn't laugh.

I continued. "Jade also said that she went to the market and all the meat was still alive. People bought something and then it got killed right in front of them."

Miss Wu still didn't speak. All this was leading to the thing that bothered me most about the stuff Jade had said. Something so terrible to imagine, so totally un-magical, that I had to know if it was true.

I moved closer and looked directly at Miss Wu. "This girl,

Jade," I told her, "she said something else. She said there are no wild birds in the whole of China. Not a single wild bird left." I couldn't express to her how horrific this was to me. The empty skies. "She said that years ago, people in China were starving. They had this ruler called Chairman Mao, and he told his people they should eat the wild birds—so they did. That's what Jade said. Even the sparrows. And I thought, is this the sort of place I come from? A country where all the wild birds had been killed and eaten so people wouldn't die?" I laid my hand on Miss Wu's arm. "Is that true?" I asked her. "Are the wild birds all gone?"

That was when the streetcar appeared through the whirling snow. It didn't start far away and grow bigger; it loomed out at us, fully formed and close up. I kept on looking at Miss Wu. Holding onto her arm. The streetcar stopped in front of us, its brakes screeching. The doors swung open. But I didn't move.

"No country is all magic, Kelly," Miss Wu said, "and you cannot dismiss an entire culture on the basis of its toilets ..."

I think she would have said more if there had been time.

"Come on, if you're coming!" yelled the driver.

I stepped on board and the doors closed behind me. I threw coins into the slot. Then I turned to look back at Miss Wu as the streetcar pulled away.

She was right, but she hadn't answered my question. The one that really mattered. Why hadn't she answered? Because it was true? Did I really come from a country where the skies were empty and all the birds were gone?

I found a vacant seat and sat down, feeling suddenly

very alone. With Raizel and Miss Wu both gone, and the streetcar on its way to the hospital, I started to think about Mom. Sure, she got headaches all the time and I'd stopped really noticing them. But she had never taken herself off to the hospital before. Was she going to be okay? Would they make her stay there overnight? And if she had to do that, who would take care of me? The more I worried, the worse the images that came into my mind. Mom with tubes sticking out of her. Mom slipping into a coma, like people did in the movies. Mom pinned under white sheets while doctors tut-tutted and shook their heads. And all the time I worried, the streetcar inched its way through the snow.

This was my first time on a streetcar alone. Sure, I'd traveled on them with Mom loads of times. And maybe it was because I had started to think about Mom that one memory from long ago came flooding back.

I was four, maybe five years old. We'd been to Chinatown, the two of us. I used to ask to go there all the time, even when I was small. That day, Mom had bought me a Chinese dragon on a stick. The streetcar was crowded on the way back, and someone gave up their seat for me. Mom stood beside the seat for as long as she could, but then more people got on and she was pushed away from me by the crowds, right up toward the front. Her smile said it was okay, she could still see me, so I was safe.

Finally, we reached the subway. The doors opened and everyone spilled out. Mom stood still, eyes locked on mine, until there was enough space for her to move back and get me. But then, when the streetcar was almost empty, a stranger grabbed my arm. An old man with a thick gray beard who stank of sweat and tobacco.

"Excuse me! Driver, excuse me!"

The driver looked back at us through the mirror.

"Driver! Look here—someone has left this little girl!"

I didn't understand why he thought someone had left me, because Mom was right beside us now, close enough to shoulder him aside.

"That's my daughter," she said, panic in her voice.

The man looked at her then back at me, puzzled. He wasn't sure what to believe. Finally, he said, "Sorry—my mistake," and turned to go.

Mom lifted me onto the platform. Instead of setting me on my feet, though, she hugged me tight—as tight as if I really had been lost. I thought I could feel her heart through all the layers of her clothes, beating hard against my chest.

When the streetcar stopped outside the hospital, I jumped off and hurried in through the nearest entrance. I walked down one corridor and then another, really worried now. I didn't know which way to go and I was too panicked to think clearly. The hospital was huge, with lots of old and new buildings connected by walkways. I found signs that said *Emergency Department*, followed them for a while, but then I turned the wrong way and the signs disappeared. I was scared maybe I'd end up at the morgue by mistake, which was very alarming because dead bodies are way scarier than sick ones.

But it wasn't dead bodies I stumbled across. It was babies. Four of them in a big room behind a glass wall. You could look but you couldn't get in. Maybe that was to stop people from stealing them. Mom says that in China, when I was born, there were more babies than parents who wanted them. But in Canada, there aren't enough babies to go around.

These babies looked so fresh and new. Like petals, crumpled and wrinkly because they hadn't finished opening up yet. Each of the babies lay in a plastic crib shaped like a milk crate. All four of them were asleep, their eyelids flickering like the eyelids of puppies when they dream.

What did they have to dream about? I wondered, moving closer to the glass. Could they remember being born? Were they recalling the feel of their birth mother's warm hands on their skin? Do these moments stay buried inside us? Are they even buried somewhere in me?

Only one of the babies had her mom and dad beside her. The parents looked down at their baby as she slept, and their faces were so totally full of love. Did anyone ever gaze at me that way when I was just a few hours old? What about a week old? A month? Six months?

Looking at those newborn babies made me angry and confused. I rushed on past, down one corridor after another, eyes blurring, not even looking at the signs. Then I stopped, leaned against the wall, closed my eyes, and breathed steadily. I tried not to think about the babies, only about my mom. I pictured her lying helpless in her hospital bed, eyes scrunched up in pain. That gave me a sense of purpose. I set off walking again until I found a sign that said

Emergency Department. And that's when I bumped into Auntie Lou.

"My goodness, Kelly, what are you doing here?"

Auntie Lou is about ten years older than Mom and very bossy. She's a high school principal and she has black hairs sprouting out of her chin. She's never been married. Raizel and I agree that the chin hairs probably have something to do with that.

"Where's my mom?" I demanded.

"Still waiting to see the doctor. I was trying to find a coffee machine. Follow me."

Auntie Lou strode off—a bossy walk, taking charge—then she halted unexpectedly and swung back around.

"Kelly—it would be a good idea for your mom to have a little peace in her life for a while. Do you understand?"

I glared at her. "No."

"I think you do. The headaches get bad sometimes. Stress brings them on. She doesn't always tell you. Like this evening, when you challenged her about your dad's swords—she could barely string a sentence together her head was so bad. Did she tell you that?"

"No."

"And she hasn't told you, either, that those swords were sold to raise money for you. She has no intention of using the funds for herself. Not even to pay bills. That money was always for you, so your mom can take you on a special March Break trip next week. To China."

It was hard not to feel a bit ungrateful when she put it like that. Even if I hated her.

Auntie Lou peered at me, puzzled. "Did you hear me, Kelly?" she said. "Your mom is taking you to China."

"I heard you."

I could have added, "I'm not going," but I didn't. This was between me and my mom. It didn't have anything to do with Auntie Lou.

"Your mom is struggling to keep things together," Auntie Lou carried on. "She is not well. And you make things even tougher for her when you insist on being so disagreeable."

I don't know why Auntie Lou thought she had the right to lecture me but, in that moment, I didn't even care, because when she said Mom was not well, all those scary pictures came into my head again of Mom weak and in pain, maybe clutching at her head, and none of the doctors knowing how to help her. Lou didn't wait for me to answer; she just hurried off through the hospital while I practically ran after her. My heart was thumping. If something serious was wrong with Mom and she died, it would be my fault for stressing her out; that's what Auntie Lou had said. I would be the one to blame. What kind of a monster kills her own mom? Maybe my birth mother did the right thing to get rid of me. If Mom died because of me, then Dad would have a reason to stay away forever. If that happened, who would take care of me?

Lou strode through the swing doors into the Emergency Department and I followed behind. Just inside the waiting room, I stopped, looking around. Mom was standing next to the bottled-water vending machine. She was wearing her favorite slacks and munching on a bag of Cheezies. She'd even had time to touch up her makeup. She saw Auntie Lou before she saw me, and turned eagerly toward her, saying something in an animated voice and then laughing louder than you are supposed to in a hospital.

Lou said, "Look who I found wandering about. Kelly, come over here."

Mom barely even looked at me. "The headache has completely gone," she said to Auntie Lou. "We'll be hours if we stay here. Let's go home."

They turned together toward the exit, not even looking behind to see if I was following. And I was glad they didn't because right at that moment, I burst into tears. Partly it was relief because Mom was okay. But I was crying out of frustration, too, because Mom had made me worry for no reason at all. Moments ago, I'd thought maybe she might die and it would be all my fault. And now here she was, acting like I wasn't even there. Didn't she care how frightened she had made me? Did she do all this—coming to the hospital, calling me up at Raizel's and everything—just to make me worry?

Mom was fine. More than fine. She looked great.

That night I chatted with Raizel online and told her everything.

According to Loopy Lou, I wrote, *Mom needs to get her feelings considered because of the headaches. But what about my feelings?*

There was a pause. *Will u go?* Raizel wrote me back.

I was still thinking about Mom and what had happened at

the hospital, so at first it wasn't clear to me what she meant.

Where?

China, stupid. Will u go?

It was funny how she still kept asking, when I'd told her the answer to that question already.

I thought about the babies I had seen earlier that evening. Where was I in the hours and days after getting born? Had anyone ever loved me in China the way that mom and dad loved their new baby back in the hospital? Truth was, I didn't know.

Mom had told me all about her China plans as Auntie Lou drove us back from St. Joseph's. "It'll be just the two of us," she had said. "A little adventure!" She told me she had planned for us to fly first to Beijing and then down to Yangshuo. There was a long silence when she finished going on about it all. I knew that Mom and Auntie Lou were both waiting for me to say something but, really, I didn't know what to say. So I just stared out the window of the car the whole way home.

Mom was going about this all wrong, running my life and not letting me decide stuff for myself. But she was right about China. I had always wondered where I came from. I did want answers. I wanted to know if it was true that there were no wild birds left in the whole of China. And I wanted to know so much more as well.

My fingers hovered above the keys.

One decision to make, then no turning back.

Yes, I told Raizel. *I'm off to China.*

I sent the message before I could change my mind.

There was a pause. Then Raizel replied.

Will you look for your birth parents?

Her question caught me completely off guard. Raizel obsesses about that kind of stuff. She never got to meet her own dad, but she's built him up to be this incredible superhero, even though everyone else can see he must have been a total loser to walk out on her mom when she was pregnant. I wish I could see my own birth parents the way Raizel sees her dad, but I can't. What sort of parents abandon a baby?

Dad told me a long time ago that it's practically impossible for kids from China ever to find their birth parents, but even if there was a way, I wouldn't do it.

Enough was enough. I was done with Raizel's questions. I snapped the laptop shut, snuggled up among my panda stuffies like I was five years old again, and tried to sleep.

5
Family

To: director@sherwoodprod.com
Subject: I have to go away for a while

Dear Dad,
It's Saturday night, and tomorrow I'm going to China. For real. So that's where I'll be if you want to find me in the next few days.

I'm kind of anxious about this trip, and you are the only person who would understand. Raizel thinks China is a cool place to visit but, to me, it's where I got abandoned, and where I waited in an orphanage for months and months without parents or even a proper name. That's very confusing stuff. I could be walking down a street and people I'm related to might walk past without me even knowing. That's strange, don't you think? So tons of things worry me about this trip, including the thought of all those empty skies. A place where every single wild bird has been eaten can't be good, can it?

I've sent you so many emails now. Ten, maybe more. I wish

you'd email me back. I need to know why you went away. You didn't even say goodbye. Trying to figure out reasons for that makes me kind of crazy. It's not that I mind waiting, Dad, if I know you will come back soon. But I keep wondering, what if you are in trouble? If that's the case, it isn't enough for me just to wait. Maybe you need to be found. Only the problem is, in just a few hours I'll be on a plane to China. And then it will be too late for me to find you. It will be too late for me to do anything at all.

Suddenly, I thought of something. There was a way I could maybe find out why Dad had left. A way to look for any clues he might have left behind. Quickly I added, *Your daughter, Kelly*, pressed *Send*, and snapped the laptop shut.

I opened my bedroom door and peeked out. Mom had finished her packing hours ago and she was watching TV in the living room. *Coronation Street*, I could tell from the voices. One of the British soaps we used to watch with Dad.

I ran downstairs, unlatched the door to the basement, and slipped inside.

Our basement stinks of mold. There are giant centipedes hiding in the corners and cobwebs that catch in your hair. But the basement was where Mom stored our unwanted things. Toys and books I'd outgrown, old furniture, clothes she couldn't squeeze into anymore. And boxes filled with all my dad's personal stuff.

We'd had a pretty big fight on the night Mom packed his things away. Dad had only been gone for two weeks.

Two weeks! I couldn't believe she was clearing out his stuff so soon. One-half of their closet. Dad's sock drawer. All his martial arts and acting books. His shaving things from the shelf in our bathroom. I stood at the top of the stairs and screamed at her as she stuffed everything into the boxes.

"Why are you giving up on him?" I yelled. "How can you just wipe him out of your life? Did you even love him?" Mom didn't stop, though. She finished packing the boxes, then she hauled each of them downstairs. I watched, and yelled, and didn't lift a finger to help.

After it was all finished, Mom walked past me with her head hung low, like she knew what she had done was shameful. She went into the kitchen and shut the door behind her. Then she opened a bottle of wine and drank glass after glass, while I sat on the stairs by myself and cried.

That night taught me a few things about my mom, I can tell you.

Even though the basement was stuffed with junk, it wasn't hard to find Dad's things. Mom had dumped his boxes right in the middle of the floor as if she couldn't bear to handle them a second longer than she had to. I counted seven. Was that all Dad had to call his own after years and years of living here?

The first few boxes were full of clothes. All Dad's shirts were crumpled because Mom hadn't bothered to fold them. As I rummaged through everything, the basement filled up with his scent—Aramis aftershave mixed with greasepaint and mothballs from the studio. I kept looking over my shoulder, half expecting to see him standing there behind me.

After the clothes, just three more boxes remained. I wasn't sure what I was looking for. Just something among all his personal and private things that might help me figure out where Dad had gone. And why.

A lot of the objects in those last few boxes made me kind of sad. I found bundles of love letters, written from Dad to Mom years before I was born. She'd packed them up with all his stuff, even though technically they belonged to her. And then I found Claude the Cat. He was the first gift I'd ever bought Dad with money of my own, a little black Halloween cat with long claws and pointed teeth. I could still remember wrapping him up in a drawing I'd done at school and dropping him on Dad's knee. It hurt to think Dad hadn't taken him, but then, what can you really take with you when everyone thinks you're just driving to the store for a carton of milk? I held Claude to my nose. He still carried Dad's scent, too. I put him aside to take back to my room.

At the top of the last box, I found a photo, creased in one corner but otherwise good as new. It was a picture of Dad and me, standing at the end of the Leslie Street Spit. The photo had been taken a long time ago; I was wearing pigtails with pink ribbons on the end. Who took it, I wondered? Was it possible Mom ever came with us to watch the herons, even though, in my memory, it was always just Dad and me? That place had only ever seemed special to the two of us. In the photograph, there were trees behind us and, in the trees, hundreds of little black smudges. Dad would know, as I did, that each of those smudges was really a heron. I'd seen the photograph before. Where, though? In Dad's wallet, that was it. So if it was special enough for him to carry around in his wallet for years and years, what was it doing down here?

I got to the bottom of the last box before finding something really interesting. Something that might actually help me find my dad. It was an address book. The old-fashioned paper kind. I flipped through it. There were dozens of names and numbers inside, all written across the lines in Dad's big, untidy scrawl. I felt a sudden rush of excitement. One of these people was bound to know where my dad had gone, and why.

I repacked the boxes quickly, leaving out Claude, the heron photo, and the address book. I wanted to get back to Mom's cell phone and start making some calls. All I had was tonight. A few hours. By tomorrow it would be too late.

"Kelly? Are you down here?"

I stood up quickly, as if I was doing something wrong.

"Kelly ..."

Mom appeared at the bottom of the basement stairs. I managed to shove the address book and the photo into the pocket of my sweater. But there was no way for me to hide Claude.

"Oh, sweetheart," Mom said, looking at the toy cat in my arms. "You must miss your dad so much." Her voice was softer than it usually was, and I had to blink away a prickling behind my eyes. Mom was holding a glass of red wine that she'd already half drained, even though it wasn't even an hour after dinner. I'd become a bit suspicious about her drinking habits, to be honest. An alcoholic mother would be the final straw.

"You can take anything of your dad's that you want," she said. Maybe it was the alcohol making her so nice. "We can look through the boxes together, if you like."

"No. That's okay."

I didn't like the way she was speaking about him. As if he was dead. I tried to move past her. "I just wanted to get Claude so I could take him to China with us," I said. "But I've still got packing to do, so I'd better go up."

"What's the rush? Hang on a minute."

Mom shoved past Dad's boxes. In the far corner of the basement there were about ten milk crates, filled with photo albums going back years and years. The way the albums were stacked was pretty messy, as if someone was in the middle of sorting through them. Behind the crates was an overstuffed chair with pink cushions. It sat on gliders, so you could rock yourself gently in it. I hadn't seen that chair for years, but suddenly I remembered cuddling up in it with Mom when I was small, reading books together before bed. When had we stopped using it? I couldn't remember.

Mom picked up an album from the crate that was closest to the chair, then she eased herself down into the glider. Wine sloshed over the rim of her glass and onto the cushions as the chair began to move, but she didn't notice.

"Look at this," she said, and opened the album halfway through. I moved forward and peered over her shoulder.

"This is your dad and me on the day we moved in here."

In the photograph, the two of them stood by the front door. Dad had his arm draped casually over Mom's shoulder. They both looked very happy.

"We bought this house because we wanted to start a family," Mom said.

I'd seen these photos before but only with Dad. And that seemed like a long time ago.

Mom turned a few more pages. "Here we are decorating the nursery," she said. The photo she was pointing to showed Dad up a ladder, inside the room that had always been mine. He was painting the walls a pastel lemon. "Your room was an office before we moved in," Mom said, "but we decided it would be for our baby. We bought a wooden rocking chair and a bookshelf with little bears on it. Your dad found an old crib at a garden sale and painted it a lovely shade of blue."

"Blue?" I asked. "I thought you knew I'd be a girl."

"This was the first time around," Mom said. I perched on the arm of the glider. "We were trying to get pregnant. Somehow we just assumed we'd have a boy—there are so many boys on both sides of our family. We were pretty optimistic, to start with. Your Dad sat by that crib night after night, dreaming of the son we would have. Waiting."

Mom took a sip of wine and handed me the glass so I could place it on the floor.

"We hoped and waited and dreamed, but no baby came. Months turned into years and slowly all our hope drained away. There wasn't going to be a baby. Our friends had families but we never would. Your dad chopped up the blue crib and together we put it out for garbage. There was so much sadness and we needed time to adjust, so we decided to go on a vacation."

Mom flipped through the album until she came to a bunch of holiday photos. In one of them there was a beautiful stone pool, more like a natural pond, really, with tropical flowers growing right to the edge and the sun sparkling on the water.

"That was our first trip to Mexico," Mom said. "We stayed at a lodge in the jungle. It was like paradise—but we were too sad to enjoy it. Then, one day, we met a couple from California. They had a little girl, maybe two years old. She looked Asian but they didn't. All afternoon we sat by the pool, watching the family play. They were so full of joy."

Mom glanced down at her wine glass. I picked it up and passed it to her. She took a sip, then held the glass away from the album so she wouldn't drip wine on the photos.

"That night," Mom continued, "we saw the family again in the restaurant. We asked the couple where their daughter was from and how they had become a family. And they shared their story with us."

Mom sipped again, then passed her wine glass back to me. I stood it on the floor. Then she carried on with her story.

"The couple said that in China, parents were only allowed to have one child. If a family was poor, they needed that child to be a boy so he could work the fields. This meant a lot of baby girls got abandoned. It's illegal in China to give up a child, so these babies were left outside schools and hospitals, places like that. The couple said there were hundreds, maybe thousands of baby girls in orphanages, waiting for a home."

"After you heard that," I said, "your grief turned back into hope."

"What?" Mom looked up at me, puzzled.

"Dad told me the story a couple of times," I said. She turned back to the album, and I leaned my hand on her shoulder, peering down.

Mom turned the page. In the next photograph, she and Dad stood together in the room that was mine now. The room that had once been an office. In this photo it looked very different. The walls that had been yellow were lilac now, and the bookcase was pink with a butterfly pattern. There was a new crib, too. A pink one.

Mom said, "That day in Mexico was the start of a new dream. We redecorated the nursery. Pinks and lilacs this time, for a girl. There was more waiting, of course, but it was exciting, because we knew that in a few months we'd have our baby."

Mom slid her arm around my waist. I slipped down a little until I was in the glider, right beside her, tight against the warmth of her body. Mom's smell was just as comforting as Dad's, when you snuggled close. Talc and lavender. I'd almost forgotten.

"This chair used to be in my room," I said.

"Yes, it did. We bought it for you."

I considered what Mom had said about that day in Mexico being the start of a whole new dream. A few months ago, I would have accepted that without question, but now I wondered if there was a more complicated truth underneath her story. Was it tough on them, settling for a daughter instead of a son? Were they ever sad that their little girl would never look like them? Everyone would always know their family was formed by adoption. Maybe they had to do some careful thinking before they decided to adopt. Perhaps it hadn't all been as sudden and as simple as she made it sound.

"And then you came to China and brought me home."

"Yes."

Mom closed the album, then moved her head sideways so it fit in the crook of my arm. It was cold in the basement, but the closeness warmed us both.

"A few days before we were due to leave," Mom said, "we got a call from our agency. A woman in Sweden had just adopted from the orphanage where you were living and she wanted to talk to us." Mom was playing with her wedding band, the fingers of her right hand twisting it round and round. It was something she always did whenever she was deep in thought.

"We called the woman back," Mom carried on, "and she told us she had just returned from China. Her own daughter was strong and healthy, but she had been alarmed at the sight of the tiny baby sharing her crib. That baby was frail and underweight. They learned the little girl's name and the name of her adoption agency. The woman said she was calling to warn us because, if our medical report said our daughter was healthy, we shouldn't believe it."

Mom paused. I waited for her to go on.

"That call was especially hard on your dad," she said. "He'd dreamed for so long of having a perfect, healthy baby, and now this. He told me he didn't think he could see the adoption through. I was so—"

"No, he didn't."

The words were out of my mouth before I could stop them. Mom stiffened. You could feel the change. Like our bodies didn't fit together anymore. Then she twisted awkwardly in the chair and looked at me.

"What?"

"Dad's told me this story, Mom, and you're lying," I said. "That's not how it was."

"Kelly, the thing you need to accept about your father—"

I struggled out of the chair. It wasn't easy because we were jammed in there together, but I did it. And then I stood up and looked down at her.

"No," I said. "It didn't happen that way." I was shaking my head furiously.

Mom looked shocked. Shocked and upset. She said, "You know that your dad was never very good at—"

"No. Mom, he told me what happened after that call. He said you were the one who wanted to back out. You weren't brave enough to take on a sick baby, but he was. When you got to China, you found out I wasn't sick at all, but if it hadn't been for Dad, maybe I'd still be living in the orphanage. You wanted to wait for a different baby, and he said no."

Mom didn't say anything for a long time. I stood there, staring down at her, wanting her to apologize because she had twisted the truth. More than twisted. She had lied. At last, Mom looked at me. In a calm and quiet voice she said, "One thing your dad has always been good at is reshaping the truth to suit himself."

I clutched Claude to my chest and ran back up the basement stairs. As I did so, my foot caught Mom's glass and sent red wine spraying up the wall. Mom called for me to come back, but I didn't. If she was going to tell lies about Dad to get me on her side, then maybe I could never, ever trust her again.

As I ran past the front door, the bell rang and I saw Auntie Lou on the other side of the frosted glass. I ignored the ringing, charged into my bedroom, and slammed the door. Then, before I could give myself time to think, I reached for Mom's cell. I flicked open Dad's address book and called the first name I didn't recognize. It had been stupid, letting Mom distract me with her phony memories, when the most important thing tonight was for me to find my dad.

"Hello?"

The voice was female and sounded elderly.

"Er ... my name is Kelly Stroud. I'm trying to find my dad and I was wondering if you might know where he is."

There was a little gasp, then the voice said, "You poor girl. You poor dear. My Frank told me all about your dad upping and leaving. I can't tell you how sorry I am."

"Do you know where he is?" I asked. "Did he say anything about going to Vancouver?"

"I'm afraid I can't help you there. My Frank and your dad have been meeting down the Fox and Fiddle every month for years. Brits, both of them. Like me. And then suddenly he stops showing up. Gone for good, a mate of his said. You poor child. If you or your mother need—"

I ended the call. For a while I stared at the address book, not really seeing a thing, just trying to get calm again. Choking back tears.

This was harder than I thought it would be.

There were lots of numbers in Dad's book I didn't recognize. And some that I did. Maybe it might be easier to call someone I knew. At least when the person answered, I'd know what to expect.

I paused on the D page. Laura Danier.

That was a name I remembered, for sure.

Laura had been an actor in Sherwood Productions for years. She had thick gray hair that fell in waves so far down her back she could sit on it. I remembered the first time I'd met her, maybe two years ago, and how she'd seemed like the most magical woman in the world.

Mom was working away a lot back then, doing the boring accountant thing she does, so sometimes Dad would take me with him to work. That summer, Sherwood was performing at a Medieval Festival in a farmer's field outside Toronto. That's where I first met Laura. She had a laugh like bells ringing, and she treated me like I was someone special, which I guess I was, being the boss's daughter. We giggled together in the pit beneath the stage, and she let me watch as she put on her costume—first the chemise, then a bodice that laced with leather all the way up her back. When Dad found us down there, he got really mad. Was she planning on doing any work? he asked. Laura shrugged, took my hand, and ran with me into the field. We danced between the market stalls as the wind whipped up her long, thick hair. Laura gathered a crowd and taught everyone a medieval circle dance. But no matter how many people joined us, I felt she was doing it all just for me.

I dialed her number. The phone rang for a really long time. Then, just as I was about to give up, someone answered. A man with a deep, gruff voice.

"Could I speak with Laura Danier, please?"

There was a pause.

"Who is this?" The voice sounded hostile.

"I'm just a friend," I said.

"No," the voice replied. "You are not just a friend. If you were one of her friends, you'd know she isn't here. So don't lie to me. And whoever you are, don't call back."

He slammed down the phone.

I sat on my bed and tried to stop shaking. It was too hard, calling people like this. How could I do it anymore? There had to be an easier way to find Dad.

Voices drifted up from downstairs. Was Mom telling Auntie Lou what had happened in the basement? Was she making me out to be a monster again?

I was still holding the address book in my hand. And tucked inside the front was my Dad's heron photograph. I looked at it for a while, then I turned it over and drew a line right down the center, from the top to the bottom. I moved to my desk, where I'd left the posting from Dad's studio door, and copied the Vancouver address down one side.

It wasn't a photograph now, I thought with excitement, it was a postcard. And I had somewhere to send it. Most likely my dad had gone to Vancouver. But why? The only person who could answer that question was Dad himself. He didn't seem to be checking his email—so I could try to contact him through the mail. The postcard wouldn't reach him for a while, but at least I'd get home from China knowing Dad had read whatever I chose to write.

It wasn't the best option, but it seemed like the only one I had. My hand hovered over the back of the photograph. Waiting while I found my inspiration. Waiting a very long time.

And no matter how hard I tried, I couldn't think of anything to say.

Not a single thing.

I dropped the pen, buried my head in my hands, and gave in to the tears.

6

Secrets

Thirteen is way too old to blubber like a kid. I wiped the tears on my sleeve and sat up straight, which was just as well, because that very moment there was a loud knock on my bedroom door. About a second later, the door swung wide and Auntie Lou strode in.

"What are you doing here?" I said, sniffing back the last of my tears.

"I came over to help your mom get ready."

"I don't mean here, our house. I mean here, my room."

"That's rather rude, don't you think?"

"This is my private—"

"Your mom might stand for cheek but I won't."

Auntie Lou probably spoke to me the exact same way she spoke to all the kids in her school. Like I was about three years old. She swept a bunch of my panda stuffies onto the floor and perched on the bed.

"You can't replace Dad, you know," I said, almost in a whisper. "So you might as well stop trying."

Auntie Lou didn't answer. Instead she said, "We need to talk."

I felt too sad and tired to argue, so all I did was wait to see what would come next. And nothing did. It took me a while to realize Auntie Lou wasn't even looking at me anymore. She was gazing over my shoulder at a bunch of drawings taped to the wall.

"Did you do all those?" she asked.

"Most of them." Having her eyeball my stuff made me kind of uncomfortable. "Raizel did a few. We're writing a graphic novel together. Not a comic book—a real graphic novel. Do you know what that is?"

"Yes, I know what that is." Auntie Lou sounded amused. Her tone had softened a little. "When you get back from China," she said, "we should discuss your choices for high school. You need somewhere with a strong arts program. You have a lot of talent, Kelly, really you do, but you need someone to—"

"I'm not going to arts school." I folded my arms to show her I meant business.

"It's not your—"

"Nope. No arts school. End of story."

I was sounding like a spoiled brat, but what could I say? That I no longer had my dad, and I didn't want to lose my best friend, too? I wanted to go to whichever high school Raizel went to. But that wasn't the sort of thing Lou would understand.

"Kelly," she said, "at what point in the past few months did you start to get so belligerent?"

"I know what that means," I told her.

Auntie Lou looked puzzled.

"The word 'belligerent,'" I repeated. "I know what it means."

"What has that got to do with—"

"When teachers use big words, it's because they think you don't understand. So it gives them power over you. But that won't work on me. I have a good vocabulary."

Auntie Lou sighed. "Yes," she said. "You certainly do. Let's save the school talk until you get back from China, then. It wasn't school I wanted to talk about anyway. It's your mom."

Whenever anyone wanted to talk about Mom, it was usually to take her side. I thought about what had happened in the basement.

"It wasn't my fault, you know. Mom was trying to say that—"

Auntie Lou cut me off. "You need to stop talking and try listening for a change."

She patted the bed beside her, like she wanted me to join her for a cozy little chat. But I wouldn't. Instead, I just slouched down further in my swivel chair and folded my arms. If she was going to talk to me like one of the bad kids at her school, then that's how I would behave.

"I need to talk to you about China," Lou said, leaning toward me as if she was sharing some big secret. "Your mom is doing this for you, because she thinks it's what you need. However, I am a little concerned. The timing is not good.

She isn't doing too well. Your mom has been under a lot of pressure these past few months."

Why was everything always about Mom? What she wanted, what she needed? It's not like Mom was blameless. If she hadn't nagged at Dad so much, he wouldn't have left us.

Lou said, "Once you leave for China, it will be just the two of you. Your mom will have no one else to depend on but you. I can't come charging over from Brantford at a moment's notice to sort things out."

So that's what she thought she'd been doing over the past weeks? Not poking her nose in our business, oh, no. She had been charging over to sort things out. Right.

Auntie Lou stood up and rummaged in the deep pockets of her ugly brown skirt. She handed me a crumpled piece of paper.

"What's this?"

"Emergency numbers. My home, cell, the school. My email addresses—work and personal. I'm giving you everything I can think of, in case you need it."

Now she was freaking me out.

"Keep that piece of paper on you at all times," Lou said. "Call collect if you need me, night or day. And remember—the two of you have to take care of each other."

She smiled, to reassure me and to show that our little talk was over. A different kind of person might have said, "Don't forget how much I love you," or something like that. Dad never ended a chat without pulling me into a big strong hug. But hugs are not Auntie Lou's style. Instead, she just turned and strode briskly out of the room.

After Lou left, I tossed some clothes in my case and dumped it by the door, then I threw on a pair of pajamas and climbed into bed. I thought Mom might come up and say goodnight. Maybe even apologize for lying to me down in the basement. But she didn't.

Long after Auntie Lou had gone home, the television kept on blaring away downstairs. I pictured Mom sitting alone in front of it, maybe feeling sad and, hopefully, a bit guilty as well. I wrapped the duvet tightly around my shoulders and tried to sleep, but there were too many worries tumbling around inside my head. I thought about the next morning and going to China, and how I had such a bad feeling about everything. Then, like most nights, I tried to reach Dad with my mind. I'd convinced myself that if only I could make him real enough inside my head, he'd sense me reaching out to him, and he'd know just how much I cared. But the thing was, as more days and weeks went by, it was getting harder to conjure him up. I was already beginning to forget the important things about him, like the exact way he tossed his head back when he laughed. I tried to feel his heavy arm resting across my shoulders, and to hear his deep voice whispering in my ear. And when that didn't work either, I tried to talk to him. The thing was, though, there was nothing left for me to say. If Dad ever did come back, I thought, he was the one who would have to do the talking. The one with a whole lot of explaining to do.

I must have dozed off because the next thing I knew, Mom's phone was ringing on my desk. I tumbled out of bed, turned on my bedside lamp, and stumbled over to answer it. There was no one else it could be except Raizel, but we'd already said goodbye, so why would she be calling this late?

"What's up?" I said.

There was a slight pause before Raizel answered.

"Can you come out?"

I looked at the time in the corner of the screen. It was ten thirty.

"Are you kidding?"

"No. This is important. Is your mom asleep?

"She's still downstairs, I think. And we have to be up really early. The taxi's ordered for six."

"Could you sneak out?"

I felt a shiver of excitement.

"Why?"

"I'll tell you when we meet."

Sneaking out wasn't something I had ever done before.

"Well? Can you?" Raizel sounded very impatient.

"I don't know. I guess."

"Do it, then. This is important, Kelly. I promise. Or I wouldn't ask. There's something I need to give you. Let's meet halfway, at the 7-Eleven."

"Raizel, what—"

"Soon as you can. Okay?"

And she was gone.

This wasn't the sort of thing Raizel usually did, even though she could be pretty dramatic at times. Sneaking out felt risky and wrong and exciting, all at the same time. I threw on jeans and a sweater and grabbed my backpack.

Then I tucked the heron photo into Dad's address book and tossed it inside. Something to show Raizel.

I crept downstairs and peeked into the living room. There was an old movie on TV, one of the romantic ones Mom likes to watch when she's all by herself. She was sprawled out on the sofa in front of it, fast asleep, and the lights from the television flickered on her face. There was an empty wine bottle on the rug beside her. Mom looked small and kind of vulnerable, curled up on the sofa like that. I hoped she wouldn't wake while I was gone. If she checked my bedroom and found it empty, she was really going to panic, and it didn't seem nice to do that to her. Even after she had told me lies.

I closed the door silently, then grabbed my coat and boots. Mom's suitcase was waiting in the hallway, packed and ready to go. I stepped over it, eased open the front door just enough to sneak through, and ran out into the night.

It wasn't snowing anymore, though the air was freezing cold. A huge moon shone brightly overhead, and the stars looked closer and more dazzling than I'd ever seen before. The street was deserted, and the only sign of life was the lamplight that glowed behind curtains as I hurried along the sidewalk. Sometimes I'd catch sight of someone on the other side of a window as they moved across a room. I imagined couples relaxing together while their kids slept peacefully upstairs. Normal families, safe and secure. A world I didn't belong in any longer.

Even if this thought was a bit depressing, it felt amazing to be outside late at night. No one knew where I was, and that was totally thrilling. I hadn't known it would feel like that. The world seemed different. Filled with mystery and excitement. It didn't seem so important now, that Mom could find my room empty and have a total freakout. This wouldn't take long, so even if she got worried, she'd soon find out that I was okay.

I started to run, my feet skidding along the icy sidewalk. When I reached the 7-Eleven, Raizel was already waiting inside.

She was standing by the Slurpee machine, leaning back on the window. Her hands were jammed into her pockets, and she had a thick scarf wrapped across her face like a disguise. I walked over.

"What's going on?" I asked her. "Even for you, this is pretty weird."

It was bright inside the store underneath the florescent lights. I blinked a few times and rubbed my numb fingers. The 7-Eleven was empty except for the guy who worked there. He was slumped over the counter, watching a movie on his iPad. A film with gunshots and a lot of explosions.

"How are you feeling?" Raizel asked in a voice that was almost a whisper. She was smiling strangely.

"What do you mean?"

"How are you feeling about China, Kelly? Tomorrow! Are you excited?"

"You know how I feel about China. I've told you, like, a million times."

Raizel leaned toward me, as if she was about to share a deep, dark secret. "Kelly," she said, "this trip could change your life."

Okay, so now I was getting irritated.

"Is that the reason you got me to sneak out? So you could tell me China might change my life? Raizel—"

"No. Not just that. Listen."

Raizel grabbed me by the shoulders and stared into my eyes. To her, this was something big. Something she'd been thinking about for days, maybe.

"While you're in China," she said, her tone suddenly serious, "try to pay attention to your senses. Like—say there is the smell of a food we don't have here, or the shape of a tree that doesn't grow in Canada—these could have been part of your life in China as a baby. They could be buried somewhere, deep down in your memory. You might have some kind of flashback. You never know."

"Raizel," I said, "remember, I wasn't even a year old when I left China."

"It makes no difference. They've done scientific tests on babies, and they remember all kinds of things. I saw something about it on TV. You just need a trigger to unlock it all."

I remembered the newborn baby at the hospital, the one with the parents gazing down at her. If my birth mom had ever looked at me like that, would the memory still be inside me somewhere?

"That's just crazy," I told Raizel. "Please tell me this isn't why you made me sneak out? It's the middle of the night!"

"No. I told you. There's something I need to give to you. This."

I hadn't noticed before, but she was holding a large

brown envelope under her arm. The envelope was bulging, so it probably had a thick wad of papers inside. She turned it over in her hands, then passed it to me, almost hesitantly. It was sealed shut and the ends wound up tightly with several layers of tape.

"Is it a gift?" I asked.

Raizel shrugged. "I guess. Sort of. Well, not really. I wanted to give it to you yesterday but it wasn't ready."

"Something you bought?" I turned the envelope over in my hand.

"No. Not bought."

"You made it for me?"

"No. Well, sort of. It was made, yes, but I had to get some help."

A car raced past the window, tires screeching as it took the corner too fast. In the distance, I heard police sirens.

"What's inside?" For some reason I was whispering now.

Raizel hesitated.

"I can't tell you,' she said, lowering her voice to a whisper, too. "But you have to promise you'll take it with you to China. And you mustn't open it until you get there, okay? There's a letter inside that explains everything. Then, you'll have a decision to make. Maybe you'll just toss everything into the nearest garbage. If you really want to do that, fine. But at least you'll have a choice."

Raizel glanced over my shoulder at the clock on the wall. I wondered if her mom knew she was meeting me this late, or if she'd sneaked out, too.

"Why can't I just open the envelope now?"

"Because you'll get really mad at me, that's why. You won't understand. You'll think I'm being ... well, dramatic."

"I already think that."

"Well, I know, but I don't want us to fight, because I'm not going to see you for more than a week, and you're my best friend. So don't open the envelope 'til China. Okay? Just do this for me."

"You're talking like you're in a movie, you know that?"

Raizel shrugged. And suddenly I realized how much she mattered to me. Raizel was the best friend I'd ever had. She put up with me even when no one else would. And if this was important to her, then I would do it, even if it didn't make much sense.

"Thanks, Raizel," I said. Then I hugged her. She looked pretty surprised because that's not my style usually, but I think she was pleased.

Outside the window, a police car rushed past and, in the same instant, we heard gunshots. The shots were coming from the iPad over on the counter, but that didn't stop us jumping almost out of our skins. We grabbed hold of each other and giggled. Then there was silence again and neither of us seemed to know what to say.

"I wish I could meet my dad," Raizel said at last. It was a strange thing to come out with, because we'd been talking about China and not about dads at all. The reflection of her eyes in the glass met mine. "Can I tell you something?"

I nodded.

"You won't laugh or anything?"

"I won't laugh."

Raizel took one glove off and studied her fingernails. Most of them were chewed up pretty bad.

"You know last year, when me and my mom went on that cruise to the Caribbean?" she said. I nodded. I'd been pretty jealous at the time. Raizel continued, "All I could think of was that my dad came from somewhere in the Caribbean. So I swiped one of Mom's old photos to take with us."

"A photo of your dad?" I asked.

She nodded. "It was taken when they were first dating. My dad was standing under a palm tree, holding a fancy drink. Mom doesn't have many photos of him, but that one's my favorite because he has such an adorable smile." She gave an embarrassed laugh.

"Go on."

"Well, the entire time we were on holiday, everywhere we went, I'd hold his photo up to all the people we met. Even strangers who passed us on the streets. Just in case one of them was him. The odds of finding Dad on that holiday were pretty slim, I know. But there was a teensy chance, and that made the trip even more exciting."

Raizel had never known what it was like to have a father. I'd had one for most of my life, until he left suddenly. Which was harder? I wondered.

Then something occurred to me. I held the envelope out to her.

"Does this—whatever it is—have something to do with my dad?" I asked.

Raizel shook her head. "No," she said. "Sorry. I didn't mean you to think that. It's nothing to do with him."

"Then what—"

Raizel glanced up at the clock again, then she leaned forward and prodded me in the shoulder.

"Have a great time in China," she said. "Don't forget to take that envelope, no matter what. And you better not open it until you get there, because you promised."

She glanced one last time at the package in my hand, then headed for the door.

"Raizel?"

She turned around. I hesitated, looking for the right words.

"If we couldn't see each other every day, or even every week or month, would we still be best friends?" I asked her.

Raizel looked puzzled. "Course we would," she said at last. "Dumb question, or what!" Then she pushed open the door and ran out into the dark.

The man behind the counter looked up from his movie as Raizel left. "Are you buying anything?" he asked me.

I thought for a second.

"Do you sell stamps?"

"Sure do."

He reached into a drawer and slapped a little book of stamps on the counter in front of me. I paid him, then took the photo-postcard out of Dad's address book, and pasted a stamp into the top right hand corner, above the address. For a long time I stared at the blank left side, just thinking. Making up my mind. Wanting to be sure. And then, at last, I started to write.

Walking home slowly in the cold, I thought over everything that had happened in the last few hours. Mom, with her lies and her slopping glassful of wine. Auntie Lou, and the emergency numbers she had written out for me to take. And Raizel, with the mysterious envelope I wasn't allowed to open until we reached Beijing.

Was China a dangerous place? I wondered. Auntie Lou seemed to think so. But even if it wasn't, the next eight days would be a total unknown. Anything could happen. In just a few hours, everything familiar would be gone and, even though the strangeness of it all scared me, I had to admit, it was starting to feel pretty exciting as well.

At the end of our road, I stopped at the mailbox, pulled back the slot and then paused, reading over the words I'd written on Dad's postcard.

The idea had come to me when I remembered what Mom had said about our tickets in the email to Auntie Lou. We were flying direct from Toronto to Beijing but, on the way home, we would be making a stopover.

Dear Dad, I had written on the left-hand side of the post-card in huge, sprawling letters. *I will be arriving in Vancouver on March 22nd on a flight from Beijing. Please meet me at the airport. I'm coming to live with you.*

I hesitated. As soon as the postcard disappeared into the mailbox, there would be no changing my mind. No turning back.

Then I let it go. The slot swung shut with a loud clang.

I ran the whole rest of the way home.

Part 2

中国
CHINA

1

外国人

FOREIGNER

Take-off the next day was pretty memorable, and all because of the man with the bald head.

"This is my first time on a plane," he said, moving into the aisle so the two of us could get to our seats. Mom knew I always liked to sit by the window. I fastened my seatbelt, then pulled out Raizel's envelope and stared at it. The mystery was eating away at me. What could it be?

"Sixty years old today," the man chattered on, "and never flown before! What do you make of that?" He smiled at us both. He was pretty fidgety. Perhaps the excitement was making it hard for him to sit still.

"Happy birthday," Mom said.

"Thank you very much!" The man moved his tray table up and down a few times as if he was trying to figure out what it was. Then he turned toward us again. "This trip's a birthday present to myself," he said. "My daughter moved to Beijing after college. That was eight years ago. We had our problems back then, for sure, but not a day's gone by that I haven't missed her. Now there's just a few hours to go, and she'll be waiting for me in the airport."

I wondered how it might feel to not see your dad for eight whole years. The thought made me feel panicky inside.

"Would you like to swap seats?" I asked him. "You should get the window if this is your first time flying."

"Really?" He leapt up, his face shining, and we all switched around.

Taking off, it was like I was seeing everything through his eyes. The way the ground disappeared from under the plane as we rose into the air. Lake Ontario, sparkling below us, then tipping up as we banked to one side. The man gasped a lot, gripping the arm rest so tightly that his knuckles turned white. As the plane climbed into clouds, he looked over at us with the biggest smile ever. I thought, this is magical for him because he's never done it before, and because he has so much to look forward to. Just like me. I had no idea what China was like. This trip was going to be an adventure, it really was. Mom might have booked it without telling me, but that didn't matter now.

Even better than China, though, was the thought of what would happen when the holiday ended. I was finally going to see my dad again. In Vancouver, at the airport. In just a few days.

The clouds parted and, all at once through the window,

we saw Toronto. Sunshine and ice made it glitter, as if the skyscrapers had been rolled in jewels. The bald man actually gave a squeal, pressing his fingertips against the window. Our city, I thought. But then I realized something. This wasn't my city any longer. No one knew it yet except for me, but I wasn't coming home.

Mom leaned close. "I was proud of you just now," she said. "Giving up your seat was a kind thing to do."

Why did she have to say something nice about me, right when I was thinking of what I had planned? Mom wouldn't be proud at all if she knew about the postcard. I was going to go live with my dad, and I hadn't told her. To put it another way, I was about to abandon my mom. Abandon. The word I hated. The thing people had done to me. And now I was planning on doing it to her.

The seatbelt sign blinked off.

"I need the washroom," I whispered.

I squeezed past Mom and practically ran down the aisle.

In the tiny bathroom, I stood and stared at myself in the mirror. I was a bad person. I should not have sent that postcard. What sort of person does a thing like that, in secret, on the sly?

I breathed deeply, pushed back panic, and tried to reason with myself. People left each other all the time, didn't they? My birth parents had done it to me. And Dad walked out on us without a word. Then there was Raizel's father. That showed it wasn't only our family, it was everyone's. Just the way life worked. All over the world, people leaving other people behind. Why should I feel bad about leaving my mom?

The pilot's voice came over the speaker system right then, telling everyone to sit down because of turbulence, and I had to head back to my seat without feeling any calmer. I stumbled down the aisle, reaching our row just in time to see Mom lean over and take hold of Raizel's envelope.

"What are you doing?" My words came out louder than I had wanted.

Mom slid out of her seat to let me back in, but I didn't move.

"Why are you touching my stuff?"

"Sit down, please," Mom said in an almost-whisper.

"Were you going to open it?"

"Lower your voice, Kelly. You're making a scene."

"It's mine. Give it back." I snatched the envelope from her and thumped down into my seat.

Mom leaned over. "I only wondered what it was," she said. "It was sticking out the top of your backpack. An envelope like that is a strange thing to be carrying in your hand luggage. I was curious."

"You get to have your secrets," I told her. "Why shouldn't I have mine?"

I wondered what Mom would do if she found out about the postcard. Not if, but when. Was she going to be mad at me, or would she just feel very hurt? How would she cope with me gone? The guilt crept back. Mom had her secrets, for sure. But maybe the secrets I was keeping were far worse that any of hers.

"It's from Raizel," I told her. "Just drawings, probably." As I said that, I realized it was most likely the truth. The envelope probably held drawings that Raizel had made just for me. Cartoons of the two of us standing next to giant pandas, or climbing up the Great Wall. That was the kind of thing Raizel would do. The sort of gift she would give. And although hand-drawn cartoons were always cool to have, the envelope didn't seem so mysterious anymore.

A while later, the cabin crew came around with drinks and little packets of pretzels. Mom ordered wine and got a Coke for me. She waited until after the cart had moved on, then she said, "Would you like me to tell you a bit about our trip?"

Anything to take my mind off Dad, and secrets, and all the other stuff. I nodded.

Mom reached into the bag at her feet and brought out a Michelin travel guide. She showed me a map of China and pointed to Beijing. "We're pretty much repeating the itinerary your dad and I followed when we came to bring you home," Mom said, "though we have less time, because I don't want you missing much school." She flicked through the guide until she got to a page filled with glossy photos of Beijing. Tiananmen Square, the Forbidden City, photos like the ones in our album back home. "We'll have a couple of days in Beijing," Mom carried on, "then we fly down to Guangxi Province, where your dad and I first met you."

"Guangxi Province? Where's that?" I was kind of reluctant to sound interested, though it was a bit pointless trying to hide it now. Mom flicked back to the map. It was in the south of China, a long way from Beijing.

"Yangshuo is in Guangxi Province," Mom said, "and that's where we're going to stay. We'll do some sightseeing, then visit the village where you came from, and see your Finding Place."

I looked up at her, shocked. "My Finding Place? You never told me we were going there."

Dad had explained to me, years ago, what a "Finding Place" was. It was the name they gave to the spot where you got abandoned. That's your Finding Place.

"Why do we have to go there?"

Mom said, "Your Finding Place is the closest you will ever get to where you came from. It's important for you to see it."

That sounded like pretty heavy stuff. Going to visit the spot where my birth parents had left me. Standing right there, just a short walk away from where I was born, maybe in the actual village where my relatives still lived. Why did Mom keep doing this to me?

Mom said, "Are you okay?"

I shook my head. I really wasn't. Not okay at all.

"I feel sick."

"Really? Oh, sweetie ..."

Mom started to rub my back gently, in circles, the way she had when I was little. Only that didn't make me feel any better at all.

The *fasten seatbelt* light blinked off.

"Let me go find someone," Mom said. "Maybe they have Gravol." She slid out of her seat and walked off down the aisle.

"You okay?" The bald man pulled his head away from the window for maybe the first time since take-off.

I shook my head.

"What's wrong?"

So much was wrong, I didn't know where to start. But one thing was more wrong than everything else.

And I don't know why I told him, but I did.

"Yesterday—well, last night—I did something that I kind of regret," I said.

The man didn't ask me to explain. But he did say, "There isn't much that can't be undone, not if you put your mind to it. Trust me."

He was right. Just because the postcard was in the mail didn't make it a done deal. I could send a letter from China. Tell Dad I had changed my mind. Or I could just stay with Mom when we transferred planes in Vancouver.

We would be in China for more than a week, and I had all that time to make up my mind.

"They have Gravol, Kelly," Mom said. She leaned over me with pink pills in her hand.

I shook my head. "It's okay," I told her. "I'm feeling better." The bald man smiled, then turned back to the window.

And after that, I slept most of the way to Beijing.

While I slept, the whole world changed. My world, anyway. I woke hours later and turned my head slowly so I could see out the window. Everything familiar had disappeared as if it had never existed, and an exotic, foreign world had opened up in its place. Down below us, stretching in all directions, there was desert. The peaks of enormous yellow dunes, like an ocean made out of stone. Our plane cast a small shadow across them, shaped like a tiny flying dragon. Through the sand-colored air I saw the blur of an empty road and, a few minutes later, a cluster of bleak-looking homes. Then, endless dunes again.

"Maybe that's the Gobi Desert," Mom said. She had the travel guide open on her knee, and she was looking at the map of China. "I guess we'll be starting our descent soon." She leaned over me to get a good look out the window. The bald man was still sleeping, his mouth open wide.

"You must have been tired, to sleep all that time," Mom said. "I guess you stayed up a bit late last night."

She didn't know the half of it.

Around us, most of the passengers were sleeping. The lights in the cabin had been dimmed and the entire aircraft was silent, except for a low thrum that probably came from the engines.

Mom said, "When your dad and I traveled to China to bring you home, they upgraded us to first class. It was so luxurious. The return journey was very different. Economy class, with our whole travel group. Sixteen babies, diapers, formula, and who knows what else? We had no idea what lay ahead."

I couldn't take my eyes off the window. Desert and more desert. Alien and strange.

"Mom?"

"Hm?"

"Was it my fault things went wrong between you and

Dad? Was it all perfect until you went to China to get me?"

It's always easier to ask those sorts of questions if you don't look directly at the person you are talking to.

"Aw, sweetie, no, it was nothing to do with you."

You have to try harder than that, I thought, if you want to convince me.

I turned to look at her. What I saw made me so surprised and kind of embarrassed that I forgot all about the desert, and even about Mom and Dad fighting all the time.

"Er ... Mom?"

"Yes, Kelly?"

"What are you wearing?"

"What do you mean?"

"I mean ... what are you *wearing*?"

She'd changed her clothes while I was asleep. What she had on now was a Chinese jacket made of shiny red silk. A bright gold phoenix was embroidered down the front.

"I bought this during our first trip," Mom said, "in Beijing's Silk Market. There was never any occasion to wear it in Toronto."

I wondered if all the Chinese people on the plane had been laughing behind their hands at her as she walked back from the washroom. A Western woman trying to pretend she was Chinese. The little silk buttons barely met across Mom's chest. It was totally embarrassing.

"I don't think Chinese people wear that sort of traditional stuff anymore," I told her. "If you want to blend in, you'd probably be better off wearing jeans and a sweater, like me."

As soon as the words were out of my mouth, I wished I

could take them back. Mom looked hurt. Disappointed. Maybe that jacket reminded her of their first trip to China and how wonderful it was. Only, now I'd spoiled that for her, just like I spoiled everything else. I thought about Miss Wu, and how I'd hurt her as well. Sometimes even when things are true, they can still be totally mean and not okay to say. When did everything get so complicated?

Just before we landed, Mom went to use the washroom. When she came back, she wasn't wearing her fancy Chinese jacket anymore. She was dressed in the same plain old Canadian clothes she'd been wearing when we left Toronto. A casual sweater and a pair of jeans.

Beijing airport was big and crowded and loud. We stood in line to get our passports checked, and all around us there were posters of smiling Chinese soldiers, with captions in English that said how friendly China was. Mom had brought all my adoption papers just in case, and I wondered if they might ask me extra questions, because I'd been born in China and I didn't look like my mom, or maybe they would say, "Welcome back," because this was where I came from. But when we reached the front of the long line, the officer in charge didn't say anything at all, and he didn't ask to see my adoption papers, either. He just waved us through, as if it was no big deal.

Past customs, it was total chaos. Everyone was rushing, jostling, and yelling. People shouted at each other in harsh Chinese tones that sounded nothing like the words I'd learned in Chinese class. Mom and I lugged our suitcases through the arrivals hall and held tightly onto each other as we got pushed by the crowds through the exit doors and right to the spot where the taxis were waiting. Outside, the air stank of gas and burned rubber. In no time at all, our luggage was being loaded into the trunk of a cab, and Mom and I were clambering into the back seat. My legs were barely inside when the driver slammed the door behind us. Then there was silence, the noises of the airport all gone, just the stink of the driver's cigarette as he turned to find out where we wanted to go.

How would Mom handle this? I wondered. She didn't speak any Mandarin at all.

But riding in a taxi in China turned out to be just like riding in a taxi in Toronto. Mom said, "The Marriott Hotel, please," in English, and then, to be sure, she gave the driver a map she had printed off from the hotel website. He looked at it for a minute, then handed it back, and our taxi inched slowly out of the terminal toward Beijing.

"Mom ... look ... the man from the plane."

I saw him as our taxi pulled out. He was sitting in the cab in front of us. I was sure it was him. His bald head was tilted sideways as if he was struggling to look back at all the people still standing outside the terminal. It looked like him, and yet it couldn't have been, because he had said his daughter would be waiting at the airport to meet him, and there was no one beside him in the cab. Our bald man was likely still inside the terminal, I decided. Running into his daughter's arms. Holding onto her, while she held tight to him, because it felt so fantastic to see her dad again after all those years.

The other taxi overtook ours and sped on ahead, but just outside the terminal, as we pulled on to a highway with about a million lanes, the traffic slowed down and we caught up again. Our cab pulled right alongside his. And that's when I saw, for absolute certain, that it was him. He wasn't looking back at the terminal anymore, he was slumped in his seat, his head lowered into his hands. And there was no one in the cab beside him. No daughter. No one at all.

Hadn't his daughter known he was coming? Had she just chosen not to show up?

The traffic started to move again and our cab turned right, into lanes and lanes of fast traffic, while the other cab carried straight on. I watched it for as long as I could, until it was totally gone from sight. I knew then that I'd never find out what had happened to the bald man from our plane, and why his daughter hadn't come to meet him. And I would never stop wondering.

Beijing could have been any city in the world. I don't know what I'd expected, but it wasn't this. Our cab was exactly like the ones we have in Toronto. The traffic was just as bad as it was on the 401. Even the apartment blocks looked like city housing back home. Everything was made of concrete. The air seemed thick and gray like concrete, though that could have been the pollution. Once we left the highway, we saw people hurrying by on the sidewalks, their collars turned up against the cold. They wore brightly colored winter scarves, just like the ones my friends wore at school. We even saw a billboard advertising McDonald's, and though the writing was in Chinese, everything else was the same. It was all very familiar. Not exciting, now we were down in the middle of it all. Not exotic, and not a bit magical the way I'd hoped.

The Marriott Hotel, where we were staying, wasn't even Chinese. We have one just like it back home in Toronto. And our room was a hotel room like any other. Not even slightly Chinese-looking. Mom flopped straight down on one of the queen beds and crossed both arms over her eyes.

"I'm wiped," she said.

I thought of what Auntie Lou had told me. "Do you have a headache again?"

Mom moved her arms and looked at me, irritated. "No, Kelly, I do not have a headache again. I just traveled halfway around the world and there is a twelve-hour time difference. So I'm jet-lagged. Okay?"

She didn't have to say it like that.

Within minutes, Mom was asleep. I sat on the edge of my bed and watched her for a long time, frustrated and full of energy. I didn't know what time it would be in Toronto, but according to the digital clock on the table between our beds, it was only three thirty in the afternoon here in Beijing. Sleeping seemed kind of dumb when it wasn't bedtime, and there was a whole new country outside, waiting to be explored.

Mom hadn't exactly said I couldn't go out by myself, had she?

No. She hadn't said that at all.

If it was okay for me to do stuff without Mom in Toronto, then why not here?

The thought was pretty exciting. I didn't have to go far. Maybe not even out of the hotel if it felt too scary. Even looking round the hotel would be better than just waiting in the room until Mom was done with her sleep.

So I slipped on my coat and headed toward the door.

Just before leaving, I remembered the envelope. Raizel had said not to open it until we got to China, and we were in China now. So that meant I could open it. But exploring suddenly seemed a lot more exciting than looking at a bunch of drawings. I tiptoed back to my bed and eased the envelope into the thin gap between the headboard and the wall. If Mom started nosing through my stuff, I didn't want her to find it.

Then I left our room and went to explore.

This was China!

The hotel wasn't very interesting but, at the revolving doors, I paused. Was it safe, going out by myself? Beyond the hotel, the street looked normal enough. Just other big hotels, lots of taxis crawling past, and sidewalks pretty much empty of people. I stepped outside, passing between two stone lions, and looked up. Of all the hotels and other buildings along the block, the Marriott looked like one of the tallest. It had a lot of funny domes on the roof that would be easy to spot, even from a distance. What if I went for a quick walk, but made sure I could see those funny domes the entire time? It would be impossible to get lost.

I started to walk.

On one side of the sidewalk were the high walls of big hotels and, on the other, dead or stunted trees and several lanes of busy traffic. There were streets in Toronto that looked just like this. I kept glancing over my shoulder to check the Marriott was still in view behind me. And it always was. How far did you have to walk to get away from touristy stuff and into the real China? I didn't know.

I reached the first main intersection and stopped to gaze around.

More than anything, I wanted there to be birds in China. For Jade to be wrong. Even if it turned out China was just like everywhere else, as long as there were birds, then somehow it would be okay.

But there was nothing. No birds on the sidewalks or in the skies. No birds in the half-dead trees, either. I listened, trying to tune out the sound of all the cars, but I couldn't hear the singing of a single bird. Not one.

Nothing.

I turned first down one side street, then another, always making sure I could still see the Marriott behind me. Soon, expensive hotels gave way to shabby apartment buildings. There were lots of bicycles locked up against the railings outside. These streets had a few more people on them, walking or biking, all of them hurrying. I passed a row of restaurants and I could smell food cooking, a smell just like in Chinatown back in Toronto. Every few blocks I stopped to glance over my shoulder. The domes on the top of the Marriott were always there, poking out over the other roofs. I listened carefully. Cars, music, horns, sirens. The kind of noise that belongs to all big cities. But not a single bird.

Then, at last, I heard them.

Not twittering sparrows or cooing pigeons like I'd expected, but something far more wonderful. Bird song that sounded exotic and filled with joy—first one bird, then many birds, as the sun broke out suddenly through the concrete-colored haze of pollution, warming the air. Bird song that floated between the high walls of the old apartment buildings.

I turned at once and followed the noise.

It took me down a narrow alley between two high-rises. I turned left, then right, always following the sounds of the birds, down winding lanes filled with crooked little houses squeezed together that reminded me of ones we'd seen in Mexico: concrete walls with peeling paint, slogans plastered here and there, and maybe for a roof, nothing but a sheet of corrugated iron. There were a lot of bicycles. Hundreds of them clattering past, some pulling carts so loaded with fruits and vegetables you could barely see the top of the rider's head. An old lady crouching beside a crate of greens looked up and smiled at me. Children squatted in the alleys, smashing stones against the thin sheets of ice that still remained where the lanes were in shadow. Old men sat together in corners, playing a game with white and black counters, their faces turned into the sudden warmth of the sun.

Dad had told me about places like this, every time he shared stories of their trip to China. It was a hutong: an ancient worker-district of Beijing. The hutongs are hundreds of years old, but now most of them are being torn down to make room for modern things like high-rise apartments and offices. I'd seen pictures of Mom and Dad walking hand in hand through the hutongs, and heard tales of how Dad bought a traditional Butterfly Sword from an old man who lived behind a shop that sold dried fish and fungus.

The hutong I'd stumbled into didn't look at all like it was about to be destroyed. It was buzzing with life.

I followed the sound of the birds, further and further into the hutong. The tiny winding streets reminded me a lot of the traditional Mexican towns I'd traveled through with Mom and Dad. But something was different. At first I couldn't figure out what it was, then suddenly I knew.

In Mexico, we had been foreigners. Tourists. Gringos. Outsiders. We looked different from the locals and, wherever we went, people tried to sell things to us. Women with babies on their hips would stare as we walked by. Men would chatter to each other in a language we couldn't understand, and it was obvious they were talking about us.

But none of that was happening here. No one paid me any attention. Why? Because I looked exactly the same as all of them. Maybe our clothes were a bit different because mine were bought in Canada, and maybe if they looked at me really closely, they'd be able to tell I was a tourist, but I was Chinese and they were Chinese. Same-same. Looking like absolutely everyone around me felt strange and new and very good.

In the heart of the hutong was a square where people could gather and chat. Around the square grew stunted trees without leaves and, under these trees, basking in the sudden sunshine, more old men quietly smoking.

And in the branches of the trees were the birds.

Not free birds. Not wild birds. Tropical songbirds in woven wicker cages, singing into the sun. And when I saw them there, beaks open, hopping from perch to perch, I felt disappointed but also really happy. Disappointed because it seemed there were no wild birds, just like Jade had said. But also glad to have found this place that was so different from everything back home. Old men sunning their pet birds, while they smoked and played board games together in a very ancient part of Beijing, just as their ancestors might have done centuries ago.

I felt something tug at my coat. Looking down, I saw a small boy. He was holding an object out to me—a plastic tube—and speaking very fast in Chinese. I couldn't make sense of a single word he said. The boy must have thought I was pretty stupid, a Chinese person unable to understand simple words. Maybe the problem was that I didn't hear too well? He spoke to me again, this time talking louder, and the men under the trees looked up to see what was going on.

For a moment that seemed endless, the boy stared up at me, shaking the tube, looking puzzled, and there was silence as everyone in the square seemed to wait for me to do something. I couldn't figure out what the little boy wanted. Suddenly I felt foreign, jet-lagged, and very lost indeed.

At last the boy gave up. He ran over to the old men, holding out his tube and repeating the same words. One of the men unscrewed the top of the tube for him and handed it back. The boy opened his mouth wide and tipped the contents onto his tongue. Then he glanced over at me, a baffled expression on his face, and ran off down one of the alleys. He had only wanted me to open his candy. That was all. I felt my cheeks burn with embarrassment as I turned away from the square and went back the way I had come, out of the hutong and into the streets of modern Beijing.

Back in the lobby of our hotel, I stood for a moment among the American business people and the western tourists with their cameras slung around their necks, and I thought, where do I belong? Here, where everyone except the desk staff looks like my parents, but thinks and speaks the way I do? Or out there in the real China where everyone looks like me, even though I can't understand a single word they say?

2

惊喜

SURPRISES

To: director@sherwoodprod.com
Subject: Second day in Beijing

Dad,

You would have been so proud of me today! So much happened, and things weren't just familiar or exotic, first one and then the other, like yesterday. I connected with the real China somehow. That was because of you, Dad. You made me take Mandarin classes, and Tai Chi, and these things made all the difference today. I wish you could have been here to share this feeling. But maybe that wouldn't have been possible because you don't look Chinese like I do.

After that, everything went bad. And now, I'm kind of more confused than I've ever been in my whole entire life.

In fact, Dad, one thing that confuses me is why I bother sending you emails you don't answer, and maybe never even receive. And why I even think you'll be there, waiting for me, when our plane lands in Vancouver. I don't know what to believe in anymore.

Good night.

Your daughter,

Kelly

The first thing I'd thought about when I woke up that morning was Raizel's envelope. I hadn't opened it yet and I still didn't feel like it. The mystery of it was bound to be better than what it really had inside. Even so, I sneaked the envelope from its hiding place and quietly slid it into my backpack. Just in case I changed my mind later. Then I turned around and looked at Mom. Her face was smushed into her pillow like she'd just woken up, but her eyes were open and she was watching me.

"Where did you go?" she asked in a croaky, sleepy sort of voice. "Yesterday, after I fell asleep?"

"Nowhere."

"You went off somewhere. I know you did."

"Only to the lobby."

Mom propped herself up and went right on looking at me.

"Really?"

"Yes, Mom. Really." I flopped down onto my bed and stared up at the ceiling. "Anyway, if you were really worried about where I was, how come you were fast asleep again when I came back to the room?"

Mom didn't have an answer for that. She got out of bed and pulled on some pants and a sweater. Her suitcase was open and I could see her special Chinese jacket all crumpled up in one corner.

We took a rickshaw ride after breakfast, through the hutong. It was pretty bad. There was a loudspeaker inside each of the rickshaws and a woman yelled at us in broken English to tell us what we were supposed to see. The rickshaws kept stopping in front of people's houses so we could look in through the windows.

Yesterday I'd felt a part of this world, walking through the little streets as if I belonged. Now I was bulldozing through it as a tourist. Treating the people like exhibits in a zoo. The men and women who lived in the hutong had ignored me yesterday, but only because I sort of blended in. Today it felt like they ignored us because they didn't like us gawking at them, deciding whether they were poor or quaint, and taking photos of their lives so we could prove to our friends that we'd seen the real China. The alleys were mostly deserted, the doors of the houses closed against us. We went through the little square where the old men had rested yesterday, sunning their birds, but now it was empty, except for a boy who had a bag of toys to sell to the tourists. The toys were chickens that lowered their beaks to peck at pretend grain whenever you pulled on a string. None of the rickshaw tourists bought his chickens, but one of them reached out her arm and gave the boy a pencil with the Canadian flag on it, smiling kindly as if she thought maybe he'd never seen a pencil before.

When we got back to the hotel lobby, Mom said, "Well, that was interesting, wasn't it? A little bit of real Chinese culture?" I was about to reply with something sarcastic, but then I noticed she was squinting and standing a little lopsided, and her face was very white. I remembered what Auntie Lou had said.

"Do you have a headache? Auntie Lou said you promised her you would say something to me if you got a headache."

Mom looked at me, sort of surprised.

"Lou told you that?"

We walked through the lobby together. "Yes," I said. "She did."

I wondered if Mom was surprised at Auntie Lou for telling me, or at me for even caring that she was in pain.

Mom said, "As a matter of fact, I do have a headache coming on."

I sniffed. "A shame. We could have gone to Tiananmen Square. But you don't look like you're faking it."

Mom looked surprised. "Faking it? Why would I fake it?"

Why had I even said that? Like Mom is always telling me, sometimes I do and say things without even thinking. Words come out of my mouth all wrong.

"Just go lie down if you need to."

Mom glanced over at the elevator. She closed and opened her eyes slowly.

"Perhaps we can go to Tiananmen Square later," she said, her voice drawling like she'd been on the wine again, "after I've had a bit of a nap. Kelly, you don't need to come up to the room with me, but stay in the hotel, okay?"

I gave a very tiny nod.

"There's the pool, gift shops, a cafe. Check those out."

She turned and sort of shuffled to the elevator. Maybe I should have gone with her, but I was pretty sure she didn't want me around anyway, so what was the point?

After the elevator doors closed, I just stood there for a while, trying to decide what to do. Then I walked through the lobby to the revolving doors and out onto the street.

I did feel a little bit guilty for not staying in the hotel like Mom said. But only a bit. Mom didn't want me to go out on my own because she thought it was dangerous, but it wasn't dangerous at all. I knew that because I'd done it already. And even in the hutong, when it wasn't possible to see the dome bits on top of the Marriott, I hadn't got lost. That was because I had a very good sense of direction.

I was standing on the sidewalk just outside the hotel, trying to figure out which direction to head in this time, when a woman tapped me on the shoulder. She was really pretty. Tall, with pale skin, short black hair cut in a very trendy style, and dangly earrings. She was thin and kind of vulnerable-looking, though it was strange for me to think that about her because I was a kid and she was totally grown up—maybe nearly as old as my mom.

"Excuse me. Do you speak English?"

Her question made me smile.

"Yes."

"Oh—that's wonderful! I need help with some directions." The lady was holding a map of the area around our hotel.

That's when I realized: *she thinks I'm Chinese. I mean, really Chinese, like, living here.*

"The rest of my group went by rickshaw this morning to tour a hutong, but my flight got in late so I missed the trip. I was hoping to go there on my own. Is that possible?"

I nodded, and pointed in the direction I'd walked the day before. "You'll see much more on foot," I said, and told her to look out for the old men and the birds.

The lady smiled. "Thank you so much. You speak excellent English."

"Sure I do. I'm from Toronto."

"Oh, I'm so sorry!" She covered her mouth, embarrassed. "I shouldn't have assumed. What a coincidence, though. I'm from Toronto, too!"

She said goodbye and headed off by herself.

There was something about that lady that I liked from the very first moment. She had this way of looking happy and sad at the same time. Kind of the way I felt on the inside.

I walked off in the opposite direction, glancing over my shoulder at the roof of the Marriott. It was warmer than yesterday but, although there were a lot of cars rushing by, no one passed me on the sidewalk. Did people take taxis everywhere in China? There were lots of big hotels in this area, and maybe the tourists and business people who stayed in them preferred to travel by taxi. That was kind of a shame because there was more to see when you walked.

At the end of the wide road where all the hotels were, there was a park. Not much of one—a swing, a slide, and a small fountain in the middle of a patch of grass. But in the center of the park, a whole bunch of people were doing Tai Chi. Chen style, too, which Dad said is the most traditional and the best. I wished Dad was there to see it with me. All the people stood in neat rows, moving together, just like the two of us had, doing Tai Chi side by side for so many years. I watched them for a while, my breath working along with their moves, even though my body stayed still. I wanted to join in so badly, as others were doing, by slipping into a gap in one of the lines. But for some reason, I couldn't bring myself to do it. After a bit, I walked on.

That's when I saw the girl.

She was lying on the sidewalk just around the corner, one leg twisted under her body, and she was crying. She was all by herself and no one else was nearby to notice she was hurt. That meant I didn't have a choice, really. I ran over to help.

We never did First Aid at school, but Dad taught me a few things—like how you never move a leg if it might be broken. I totally hoped the girl's leg wasn't broken, though, because I had no idea how to call for an ambulance in China. I crouched down beside her and, as I did, she moved her leg and it straightened out just fine, which made me very relieved. I put my hand on her shoulder because, even though my Chinese was bad, this would show that I cared. She turned to look at me. She was maybe only six or seven years old and her face was streaked with tears.

There was a lot of blood. She'd cut her knee on the concrete when she fell, and the blood was running in streams down to her ankles and turning her white socks red. I took my scarf off and held it gently over the wound, pressing a little to stop the bleeding, like Dad had taught me. As I did this, the girl started talking in Chinese, at first mumbling through the tears, then speaking more clearly. Or, at least, clearly if you understood the language. Sometimes she spoke a word that seemed familiar, but her sentence would run off somewhere else before I could remember what the word meant.

But maybe it didn't matter that I couldn't understand. I smiled to reassure her, then I helped her stand up. She rubbed tears from her eyes and looked closely at me, probably making up her mind if I was safe or not. Then she said more words and pointed over to a high brick wall a little ways down the road. Her home, maybe? She put her arm around my waist so I could help support her as she limped along. The knee was still bleeding, but not so badly now. I glanced over my shoulder. I could clearly see the Marriott with its domes on top. There was no way I could get lost.

I helped the little girl along the sidewalk as far as the brick wall. A wooden door was set into it about halfway along. There was Chinese writing running down the door in bright colors, and a few posters tacked on with nails. The girl pushed the door open and we went inside.

Behind the big door was a schoolyard. The high wall ran along three sides and was covered on the inside, from top to bottom, with colorful murals that showed cartoon children with smiley faces and big eyes, dancing with colored ribbons. Everything looked new and shiny: the paint on the murals, the basketball nets, a set of orange and yellow monkey bars. The branches of trees trailed over the walls in places, some of them thick with pink and white blossoms, even though it was only March.

On the far side of the play area stood the school—a long wall of glass windows, each with a door beside it: seven or eight classrooms filled with kids, each one opening out onto the playground. Through the windows, I could see more colorful murals, brightly painted desks and chairs, and charts with huge Chinese characters in green, blue, and pink.

As I helped the little girl limp across the open space of the playground, it seemed that every set of eyes inside the classrooms turned to look at us both.

A door flew open and one of the teachers ran out. She knelt beside the little girl and examined her knee, all the time asking questions, one after the other, really fast. I could tell they were questions because I heard the word *"ma?"* over and over. This is what you use in Chinese if you want to turn a sentence into a question. But she was talking too fast for me to pick out anything else. The girl looked down at her knee and started to sob again, loudly and kind of dramatic. Maybe that was because of the attention she was getting. Her cut was still bleeding, and all the blood made it look worse than it probably was.

The teacher pointed over to her classroom and we helped the girl limp inside. Then she hoisted her up onto a desk, said something to me in rapid-fire Chinese, and hurried off.

Once the teacher had left, the children abandoned their desks and gathered around us in awed silence. They looked solemnly at their friend with her bloody leg and whispered among themselves. At last, a little boy stepped forward and tapped my arm. He said something to me in Chinese.

I hesitated. "*Qing man man jiang*," I said. Please speak slowly.

The children giggled and spoke excitedly to one another.

"*Ta fa sheng shen me shi le*?" said the boy. I replayed his words in my head. What happened to her?

"*Ta shuai dao le*," I said, trying hard to get the tones right and hoping the children wouldn't laugh. The words meant: she fell down.

The children giggled and chatted among themselves again, but they didn't seem to be mocking me. They seemed excited by the mystery of who I was. No one was looking at the injured girl anymore. They were all staring at me. But perhaps that was okay because the little girl wasn't focused on her knee anymore, either.

Now the small boy was speaking for his entire class.

"*Ni cong na li lai*?" he asked. Where are you from?

I replied, "*Wo lai zi Jia na da dan shi wo chu sheng zai Zhong guo*." I am from Canada. But I was born in China.

Again, giggles and chatter. Maybe my tones weren't totally right. Maybe the children were trying to work out what I'd said.

At that moment the teacher returned, carrying a First Aid kit. I was a bit disappointed, really. The children had understood me. I was beginning to understand them. This was surprising, and really exciting, too. I was proud of myself and I didn't want it to end. The little boy who had spoken first ran up to his teacher and said something too fast for me to catch, all the time pointing over at me. The teacher said something in a loud voice and all the children returned to their desks.

I smiled at the little girl. Her knee had stopped bleeding.

"Thank you very much," said the teacher slowly, in English, while her students looked on, awed. "We are very happy for your help."

"You're welcome," I replied. Then I realized that in thanking me, she was really showing, politely, that it was time for me to leave. I wished we could have gone on the same way all afternoon, me and the teacher and the other kids, sharing stories of our lives in broken English and Chinese.

I turned to the little girl one last time.

"*Kuai dian hao qi lai*," I said. I hope you feel better soon.

For a moment, I had been a part of something. Now I wasn't anymore.

I left the school and turned the corner back toward our hotel.

Even though I felt let down and disappointed by how quickly things had ended, something in me had changed. I'd used my Chinese and maybe made tons of mistakes, but the little kids had understood. That didn't make me one of them, but it had opened a door. I felt kind of powerful. Excited. Because if I could speak Chinese even a little bit, and understand what other people said, then so much more would be possible.

And when I saw the people doing Tai Chi on the way back, I felt different about that, too, even though maybe only half an hour had gone by. I felt as if I had a right to be there. It wasn't hard to walk slowly around to the back of the park, join one of their lines, and match my moves to theirs. No one even turned to look. I ran through the moves like I had a million times with Dad, and I thought, they don't know that I'm not completely one of them. Knowing Tai Chi is just as good as language, in a way. It's something to help you fit in. On the outside, my body moved like everyone else's but, on the inside, I was bursting with pride.

Later, back in the hotel, I saw the lady again. The tall, sad-happy one. There was a shop inside the lobby that sold jewelry, and it was full of tourists hunting for souvenirs. The lady was among them. As I walked past, she noticed me and waved. She was holding up a silver chain with a tiny jade Buddha on the end.

I walked into the shop.

"That's pretty," I told her.

"It's for my daughter," she said.

"I might take something back for my friend Raizel," I said, thinking that jade probably wasn't what Raizel would want.

The lady gave a little laugh. "My daughter isn't back in Canada," she said. "She's here. In China. Just a baby. I'll be meeting her in a couple of days."

Her words were a huge surprise to me, because I hadn't realized there would be people at our hotel about to form families like ours. I thought of her baby, waiting somewhere, probably in an orphanage, not knowing that in a few days, her life would change forever. I wondered what the little girl's crib looked like, her room, the people taking care of her, and I thought about how nothing in her Chinese life would stay in her memory; it was all going to be just a blank as she grew up.

I was so caught up in all these thoughts that, for a while, I didn't even notice Mom, striding across the lobby toward the exit doors. And when I did notice her, my first thought was: so much for a headache. But where was she going?

Mom practically fell through the revolving doors and ran out into the street. I hurried after her.

By the time I reached the sidewalk in front of the hotel, she had already disappeared around the corner. Feeling sort of like a spy, I hurried after. Just before reaching the corner, I broke out into a run, not wanting to lose her, and that's how Mom and I ended up ramming straight into one another, as she headed back toward the hotel. We stumbled apart. Mom looked at me kind of puzzled, and then relieved.

"Kelly. Oh, for heaven's sake, Kelly ..."

And that's when I realized why Mom had been practically running across the foyer and out of the hotel. Why she'd charged around the corner, only to turn back and run in the opposite direction. She was frantic with worry. She was looking for me.

If Mom was relieved to find me, the relief didn't last for long. It turned straight to anger.

"Where were you?" she screamed, grabbing hold of my shoulders. "Did you leave the hotel, after I told you not to? Where did you go?"

"I was at the gift shop, in the foyer, that's how I—"

"Enough. I'm done with all the lies."

"I'm not lying!"

"You never listen to me, Kelly!"

"Get a grip, Mom, you're making a scene."

This was not a kind thing to say, really, when Mom was out of control, mostly because she was worried about me. And it was also a stupid thing to say because it made Mom even madder.

"You can't just go wandering off! It's not safe—we're in a foreign country!" Mom yelled.

"It's not a foreign country to me."

I thought about the children at the school, and how I'd joined in with Tai Chi in the park. For a while, China hadn't seemed foreign at all.

"Don't be ridiculous." Mom dropped her voice then, but somehow she sounded even angrier. "What's wrong with you? Hm? Can you answer that, because I know I can't."

She paused a few seconds to catch her breath. But she wasn't done.

"Auntie Lou keeps saying you need a firmer hand. And I have to admit, I'm at a loss what to do with you these days."

Maybe I was supposed to answer, but I couldn't think of anything to say. In the silence, I found myself listening for birdsong again. Nothing.

Mom took a step back.

"You do whatever you want, all the time," she said. She spoke slowly, almost sadly, and her voice was so quiet, I had to listen hard to hear. "You act without considering the consequences. It's going to lead you into trouble, Kelly. I don't know what's best to do. But Lou does, and the more I think about it, the more it makes sense."

I wasn't liking the sound of this.

"What does? What makes sense?"

"Lou has asked us to move in with her. Sell the house and go to Brantford. She suggested it weeks ago. I kept saying no, even though I liked the idea, because I knew you would be against it. But you force my hand, Kelly, you really do. I can't keep doing this on my own."

"You've got to be kidding."

But she wasn't.

"Lou will help us get back on track. Moving in with her will solve the money problems. And maybe both of us will benefit from a fresh start."

This wasn't an empty threat. Mom had given this idea a lot of thought, I realized, maybe for weeks and weeks, without ever discussing it with me.

Move to Brantford.

Live with Auntie Lou, who didn't like me one bit.

Leave Raizel and everything else that was left of my life.

The idea horrified me. But then I thought: none of this mattered. I wasn't going back to Toronto, was I? After China, I'd be leaving Raizel behind, anyway, and going to live with my dad. So why was I so angry at Mom for doing this?

It's one thing to make a decision for yourself. It's another when someone else takes your life away and doesn't even ask you first.

Mom couldn't look me in the eye. She knew what she'd just done, but instead of saying sorry and trying to make things better, she walked straight past me and into the hotel.

She must have expected me to follow, but I didn't.

I turned and ran.

Down the long street with all its glitzy hotels and onto a side road, not even checking to see if the roof of the Marriott was still in view behind me. On and on, fast as I could. So fast that I didn't have to think.

Restaurants ran the whole length of the sidewalk, all of them with red paper lanterns swinging outside. I ran past them, not noticing cars, not caring if I got run over, for five minutes, ten minutes, fifteen, until all my breath was gone. Wearing down the anger. Numbing all the hurt. Just running, until my muscles ached and my sides were splitting. Until I got to a point where there was no room inside me to think because I was so busy struggling to breathe. And then at last, when it wasn't possible to run anymore, I slowed to a walk. First brisk, then sort of exhausted and staggering.

At last I came to a standstill. Beside me was a small concrete bench. I fell onto it and gasp-breathed for a minute, focusing on a red paper lantern hanging across the street. The lantern swayed and trembled. I watched it move and listened to the sound of my breathing. Then I opened my backpack, dragging out a tissue to blow my nose.

There, inside my backpack, was Raizel's envelope.

I pulled it out onto my knees and looked at it.

Sometimes it felt like Raizel was the only person left who understood me. I turned the envelope over in my hand and thought about how typical it was that Raizel had behaved so mysteriously about the envelope, when all that was inside, most likely, was a bunch of hand-drawn cartoons. She had always been so dramatic about everything. Well, right now I needed Raizel more than ever before. Sketches done by someone who cared about me somehow didn't feel like a disappointment anymore. They felt like something that would make me feel a whole lot better.

So I tore open Raizel's envelope and dragged the contents onto my knee.

But she hadn't given me drawings at all.

Inside the envelope, I found about twenty identical posters, each one filled with big Chinese characters I couldn't read. The one on the top was the original, and the others were photocopies. Raizel had attached a post-it note that said: *Just in case you change your mind.*

Change my mind about what?

There was a folded note at the bottom of the envelope. I read it out loud. It said:

Dear Miss Wu,
Yesterday, when you came into our shop for a hot chocolate, you asked my friend if she knew how to write Chinese. Well, she doesn't, so I was hoping you could make a poster for her to take to China when she leaves on Sunday. Here is what it needs to say:

Found, outside the village school, June 16th, 2001, age one day:
Baby Girl.
If I am your daughter, please call me.

I would like to meet you.
Contact me here: ____________________
Kelly Mei Stroud.

Kelly doesn't think it's important to look for her birth parents, but she might change her mind once she gets to China. If she has some posters to put up, and if she does change her mind, she can do something about it.
Thank you for doing this, Miss Wu. Kelly is my best friend.
Raizel

I had hoped to find something inside Raizel's envelope that would cheer me up. But this didn't cheer me up at all.

It made me feel even more confused.

3

宝贝

BABY

The next day, we flew to Guilin.

"We'll have time to see Beijing properly on the way back," Mom said, as we boarded the plane.

It was practically the first thing she'd said to me all morning. She was still angry at me for going off by myself, even though I'd proven it was totally safe in China by not getting pick-pocketed or lost or anything. And I could tell she also felt guilty about what she'd said on the street outside the Marriott. In bed the night before, she had tried to apologize. "Kelly, sweetheart," she had said, "about us moving in with Auntie Lou ... I really didn't mean for you to find out like that. I should have told you at a better time and then I could have explained properly. I was angry and it just came out."

I rolled over and refused to listen. She deserved to feel

bad. Let her go on thinking for a little bit longer that she could control my life. All that was going to change once we landed in Vancouver.

For almost the entire plane trip, Mom and I didn't say a word to each other. Mom sat with her head down, staring at her hands as if they were the most interesting thing in the world. I leafed through the in-flight magazine even though it was mostly in Chinese, flicking the pages noisily. Finally, as we started to descend, Mom did what she always did when there was a bad atmosphere and she couldn't bear it any longer. She took a deep breath and started to chatter.

"Guilin is a big city like any other," Mom said in a voice that was loud and falsely cheery, "so we'll take a taxi from the airport, straight to Yangshuo. We're staying in a place called the Li River Inn. That's not the hotel your dad and I used when we came to bring you home—but it looks even nicer. You know, Kelly, you come from one of the most gorgeous provinces in China."

I doubt my birth parents cared whether their province was pretty or not. They were probably too busy trying to grow enough food to stay alive. And it hardly made a difference to me in the orphanage because most likely the babies never got to go outside. So why did I care that I was born somewhere pretty? I was too busy wondering whether there was already a *For Sale* sign outside our home.

"We'll spend time at the inn," Mom chattered on, "enjoying the views and relaxing. Then we'll explore. There's so much to do!" I gazed out of the window. The city we were flying into looked gray and very boring from the air. Mom continued, her cheery voice sounding even more fake. "We can travel down the river on bamboo rafts. Take a trip to the rice paddies. And we can go see the village where you were born. Look for your Finding Place. We only have three days, but maybe we can even visit your orphanage."

She stopped with the awkward chatter all of a sudden, and placed a hand gently on my shoulder. Reluctantly, I turned around.

"Everything will work out, Kelly," Mom said. The false cheeriness was gone, and her voice sounded so kind and full of concern that it made me want to scream. "Try not to let things spoil our trip. This was supposed to be bonding time for the two of us. Something we badly need."

"You can't make me live with Auntie Lou," I said.

Mom sighed, kind of giving up on me. "We're on holiday," she said. "Let's just enjoy what we have right now, and wait and see what the future brings."

Wait and see. One of her favorite phrases.

Wait and see.

I shrugged away Mom's hand and shifted sideways again to stare out the window.

An hour later we were in a taxi, heading out of the airport and through the city.

Guilin was big and busy for sure, but it wasn't at all like Beijing. The buildings weren't as tall, and they were older and more crumbly looking. It was warmer in Guilin because we were further south, and the driver drove with his elbow hanging out the window, so all the noises of the city wrapped themselves around us, the honking of cars and the sound of people shouting, laughing, playing music. There were tons of bikes, and traffic lanes didn't seem to be marked, so the cars and cabs and bikes had to weave all over the place, in and out of each other, though everyone seemed to know where to go and none of them crashed. Our taxi drove through what looked like a market, and crowds of people parted so we could get by. At an intersection, we stopped for a red light. A very old man on a bike pulled up beside us. The back of the bike was piled high with more sacks and boxes than you would ever think possible. The man chewed on a piece of sugar cane. He turned his head and smiled at me through the window. Most of his teeth were black, but he still had the kind of smile that lights up an entire face.

Then we left the city behind and everything changed.

We moved silently along a brand new highway that ran right through the middle of the strangest mountain range I'd ever seen. These mountains looked just the way a child would draw them—pointy as a witch's hat—and there were thousands of them, stretching into the distance on both sides of the road. The mountains closest to us were lush and green, covered in trees. Between them, the peaks further away seemed to fade off into mist. Those hills looked like they belonged in a fantasy movie—maybe something like *The Hobbit*—and not in the real world at all. You could imagine dragons living in lairs deep inside them, in caverns full of treasure.

"Karst formations," Mom said. "You'll find scenery like

this almost nowhere else on earth." Through the rearview mirror, the taxi driver caught my eye and smiled.

Driving along on the ultra-modern highway, we whizzed past villages that looked like they hadn't changed in maybe a thousand years. Tiny stone houses clustered together, with roofs that curved up at the corners like miniature pagodas. Strange beasts worked in the fields, the people leading them sometimes so bent and old they could have been there since the dawn of time.

"Those animals are water buffaloes," Mom said.

"It's another world," I breathed.

"The world you were born into," Mom said quietly.

For a whole hour we drove along the highway, and all that time the Karst peaks rose up on both sides of us. Too many for anyone ever to count. Then we pulled off, driving down a narrow, windy road that snaked between the strange hills. At the base of every peak grew giant ferns, and the only sign of human life anywhere was an occasional lump of carved stone, surrounded by plastic bottles and garbage. The stones looked just like tombs.

Then our taxi pulled up at the Li River Inn.

The inn wasn't in Yangshuo at all, at least not in the actual town. It was kind of in the middle of nowhere. The driver let us out on the side of the road. All we could see was a brick wall that was the back of the inn, and a path leading around to the front where the entrance was. Mom paid the driver and we dragged our suitcases along the path, down a set of stone steps, over an ornamental bridge, and through a garden of bushes covered in enormous red flowers.

We turned the corner and saw the place where we were going to stay.

The Li River Inn looked like it had been plucked straight out of a fairytale. It stood on the banks of the Li River, halfway up a grassy slope. It had a funny thatched roof, and there was a lovely terrace out front with bright mosaic floors, bamboo furniture, and carved wooden panels instead of walls. Behind the terrace, through arched pillars chiseled into dragon heads, I could see a pleasant restaurant, all of the tables covered in blue and white embroidered cloths. From the restaurant and terrace you could look out over the most incredible view: a winding river and, beyond that, Karst mountains that went on and on forever, holding up a perfect blue sky.

We dropped our suitcases by the reception and, for a while, just stared. It had rained a lot the night before and now the pointy hills were blurred by a light mist that shimmered when sunlight flashed across it. The Li River snaked lazily between the peaks and, here and there, a fisherman stood on a bamboo raft, sinking a long pole into the water to move himself along. The rafts drifted by at a very slow pace, as if the beauty of the landscape was so enticing that none of them could see any reason to hurry.

For a short time, at the very start of my life, this had been my home.

It was strange to think I was a part of all of this. That I was born right here, more or less. Perhaps the funny, pointy hills were the first thing I had seen when I opened my eyes on the world. I recalled what Raizel had said about early memories, and how they maybe stayed buried inside you somewhere. Were the pointy hills inside of me? The smell of them when it rained? Even the sound of birds in their trees?

Except there weren't any birds. None that I could see from here, anyway.

No wild birds in Beijing, and now no birds in Yangshuo, either.

Could Jade be right?

"It's been a long day," Mom said. "Let's go unpack."

I shook my head. "Later," I said, turning away from her. "I want to look around. That's if you don't think it's too dangerous."

Mom didn't tell me off for being sarcastic, but she did look a bit disappointed. For a second she hesitated, and I thought maybe she was going to say I had to come upstairs with her, whether I wanted to or not. But then she sighed.

"Maybe we could use a few minutes apart," she said. She took hold of her suitcase in one hand and mine in the other, and headed off up a windy staircase to our room.

I was just wondering where to go and what to look at first, when there was a sudden explosion of laughter and chatter from the terrace. The sound was so unexpected in such a peaceful place that I turned round to look. A group of about fifteen or twenty people was gathering there, all of them hugging each other, talking excitedly in too-loud voices. They had big suitcases with them and a lot of hand luggage. They spoke English and had North American accents, just like me. Most of them were couples a bit younger than my mom, but there was one woman who stood a little off to the side by herself. She was tall, with cropped black hair ...

It was the lady from our hotel in Beijing.

This seemed like such an impossible coincidence that I had to move closer to be sure. She looked shy, standing on her own among all the couples and, although some of the people said things to her, smiled at her and tried to include her, you could tell it was much easier for the other women to chat with each other, because then their husbands all had someone to be friends with as well. The tall lady was the only one on her own. After a few minutes, the group began to break up, all the people collecting suitcases and wheeling them off toward their rooms. Husbands and wives, holding hands or with their arms around each other. Groups, with the wives side by side and their husbands behind. I stood at the edge of the terrace and watched them all go, until the only person who remained was the tall lady. She turned to leave by herself, and that's when she saw me.

"Are you ... did we meet ..."

She spoke softly, walking in my direction, the same sad-happy smile on her face.

"Beijing, at the hotel," I reminded her. "You were buying a jade Buddha for your daughter."

"Tomorrow is when I meet her," the lady said. "My baby." She looked past me, through the arches, over the river and out toward the hills.

I didn't know what to say, other than how weird it was that we were both on our way here, of all the possible places in China, but that was pretty obvious. So instead I told her, "I was born here, too. My mom and dad came to Yangshuo to adopt me when I was ten months old."

"Really?" The lady looked at me like I was a movie star. "And you're here with ...?"

"My mom. She's gone up to our room. We must have been on the same flight as you, though I don't remember seeing you. Maybe my mom booked the trip through the same people you did. I dunno. It's kind of a coincidence otherwise."

"She brought you back ..."

"To see where I came from. Where I was born. Yes."

The lady hesitated, as if she wasn't quite sure what to say next, then she asked, "Are you thirsty? Do you have a few minutes to sit and chat?"

I guess if you're adopting a baby from somewhere, it must be pretty cool to meet a person whose history is the same as your daughter's, and who is now fully grown. Or almost fully grown. Me. The lady—Clare—ordered each of us a mango juice from the bar, and we sat opposite one another at a small bamboo table in the restaurant, looking out through the dragon arches, over the terrace, and down toward the pointy hills and the Li River.

"These hills are very famous, you know," Clare said. "This entire region was once a limestone plateau, far above our heads, and when the rain wore the limestone down, these strange hills were all that was left." She took a sip of her drink. "The man at the front desk says it's never usually this mild in March. Never quite this lovely. A good omen, maybe, for all of us." She turned her eyes from the view and looked at me again. "Does it feel strange, Kelly? Coming back?"

I thought about it. In Beijing, it had been kind of amazing, discovering the Chinese part of myself. But then I'd heard about us moving house and, for a while, my thoughts hadn't been on China at all. Not until I saw the Karst peaks for the first time. Now I was starting to feel this magical landscape sort of belonged to me. And it was so incredible, so breathtaking, that it felt like discovering a really neat part of myself that I'd never known existed. Soon, if Mom had her way, I'd be standing in the village where I was born, watching people walk by us and wondering if they were related to me. Any of the complete strangers who passed us might be my birth parents, my brothers, sisters, or cousins.

I said, "I feel a bit confused at the moment, to be honest."

Clare didn't respond. She was waiting for me to go on.

"Raizel—my best friend—she thinks we carry memories deep inside us of stuff that happened a long time ago. Even if we can't actually remember those things, we might hear a sound or smell something, and it can act like a trigger. We'll somehow know we're reliving an experience from our past."

"Your friend sounds wise," Clare said, and she wasn't humoring or mocking me.

"Can I see a picture of your baby?"

She brought out a beautiful silk purse exactly like one in Mom's jewelry drawer back home, and took out three passport-sized photographs. All of them were taken in front of a wall painted with frogs and butterflies, exactly like my own referral photos.

I remembered Dad telling me that the day my photos arrived in the mail, Mom had made dozens of copies in different sizes to put all over the house. She stuck them on the fridge, over the fireplace, above their bed, and even beside Dad's shaving mirror in the bathroom. When you get the referral photos, it means you know who your baby is, but you still have to wait weeks before you can travel to China. Dad said a referral photo is something the parents can begin to fall in love with. With my face plastered all over the house, he told me, falling in love was something neither of them could fail to do.

"My daughter," Clare said. "Her name will be Phoenix."

"She's beautiful!"

And she was. Thick, shiny black hair. A nose that was small and round as a cherry. Eyes opened wide in surprise at the camera as if she hadn't seen anything like it before.

"She lives in the same orphanage as I did," I told Clare.

Clare looked very surprised. "How can you tell?"

"The wall. My referral photos were taken in front of the same mural. I have copies of them in my memory box, and Mom still has one in her wallet—it's torn and crumpled now. Dad said the orphanages are mostly very poor, but they'll often paint one wall to look nice, so new parents get a good impression of where their baby is living."

Clare was holding the photographs gently in the palm of her hand, as if they were the most precious thing in the world.

"How old is she?"

"Almost eleven months."

"Same as me when I was adopted. Will you get to see the

orphanage tomorrow?"

Clare shook her head. "No. They bring the babies to us, right here."

"Mom and Dad never got to see where I'd been living, either. But Mom says we might go to visit the orphanage this week. I could take some photos for your daughter if you want."

Clare looked surprised and very pleased. "You'd do that? I'd be very grateful. So would Phoenix, one day."

"No problem."

I'd wanted to ask the next question ever since we started talking, but it didn't seem very polite.

"Where is your husband? Did he have to stay in Canada?"

Clare laid the photos of her daughter in a line on the table and didn't take her eyes off them. She stirred her juice round and round with the straw.

"My husband died," she said, "in April last year. In the same week that our daughter was born, in fact, though of course we didn't know that then. We were in a car accident. I was driving the car."

Why did she feel the need to add the last bit, *I was driving the car*? It wasn't important who had been driving. The awful thing was that her husband had been killed.

"China doesn't allow single parents to adopt anymore," Clare continued. "When my husband died, we had already been waiting five years for our referral. It takes much longer these days than when your parents adopted. I was afraid that losing my husband would mean losing my daughter, too. So a few weeks after the accident, I wrote a letter and had it translated, and the agency mailed it to China for me. In the letter, I told them what had happened and asked them to let me continue with the adoption as a single parent. I guess whoever read my letter must have had some compassion. They let me stay in the program."

I didn't know what to say. Clare was talking to me as if I was a grown-up, but I had no idea what it was you were supposed to say to someone who tells you a story like that.

"I'm ... sorry that your husband died."

It was all I could think of.

"Me, too."

Clare swept up the photos and tucked them back into their silk pouch. "Just a few hours left until I meet my daughter," she said, with one of her sad-happy smiles.

Those smiles made sense now.

Clare leapt to her feet, as if it was up to her to lighten the conversation, regardless of the effort it took.

"You have lovely hair," she said, moving around the table to stand behind me. "Almost—yes—natural chestnut highlights. A little auburn, even, under the light. May I?"

She let my long hair trail through her fingers.

"Are you a hair stylist?" I asked.

"I own three salons in the West End," she said.

"That's where I'm from—near High Park," I told her.

"One of my salons is on Roncesvalles."

"My friend Raizel lives near there!"

"Really?"

Clare lifted her bag from under the table, opened the clasp, and fished inside for something.

"Would you like braids?"

"Sure!"

And so we sat there like a mother and daughter for nearly an hour, chatting about Toronto while the Karst formations turned first pink, then a dozen blazing colors, and the sun dropped lower in the sky. Clare did my hair in French braids and described all the things she wanted to share with Phoenix in the years ahead.

"You'll make a great mom," I told her.

I wondered: had anyone ever said that to my mom, in the days before some stranger placed me in her arms? Most likely they had. And now, quite probably, my mom was sitting alone in our hotel room, wondering where I'd got to, and puzzling over everything that had gone wrong between us. I knew that because I know my mom. But knowing it didn't make me go upstairs so we could talk. I suppose I was punishing her. If I had to spend every day with Auntie Lou, it would be like a living nightmare for me. Mom knew that, but she had still planned to make it happen.

"Clare—listen!" I whispered, just as she finished the braids. I stood up and walked toward the white railing that separated us from the terrace and the bizarre mountains beyond. Clare came to stand beside me.

"What is it?"

At first I wasn't sure, because it came from so far away, up between the peaks that glowed a deep mauve now, in the setting sun. Then I heard it again.

I was absolutely sure this time.

From somewhere far up among the strange, pointy hills came the sound of birds singing.

4

真相

TRUTH

Bells woke me up at dawn the next day. Soft, jangling bells like the ones a farmer might tie around the necks of his cows. I snuggled under the covers and listened to all the unfamiliar noises in this land that was so strange and magical and yet, in a way, belonged to me. Below our hotel window, the voices of children began faintly, grew louder, then faded away. Weak yellow light seeped through the shutters and into our room.

Mom was still asleep, her face pressed into the pillow and one arm trailing over the edge of her bed. I thought about Clare and wondered whether she had managed to sleep. Had she spent the night standing by the window of her room, waiting for the mountains to turn from black to gray, and the new day to come?

Today, Clare and Phoenix would become a family.

What had my own parents felt like in the hours and minutes before a stranger put me in their arms? I knew Dad well enough to guess he probably slept that last night like it was any other. He was pretty practical about those kinds of things. I could almost hear him saying to my mom: "We'd better get a good night's sleep, love. It could be our last one for a while."

But what about Mom? She got stressed by things pretty easily. Maybe that's why she had so many headaches. We were both emotional people, which was a big part of our problem.

No. Mom would not have slept at all the night before.

And me? Where had I been, as Mom waited anxiously to meet her daughter? The thing about being adopted is that there's a part of the picture that's always a blur. It's your parents' story you know, not your own. I've heard so many times how my mom and dad waited in the lobby of their hotel for me to arrive. I can even tell you that the lobby had a lot of potted trees and plastic orange chairs. The babies were late, so everyone got pretty anxious. Then, suddenly, they were there. We were there. More than a dozen of us in the arms of orphanage staff, wailing and confused.

I've heard this story so many times that the picture inside my head is detailed and real, yet I don't have the slightest clue how I got to that hotel. Did they bring the babies in a bus or several cars? What kind of crib had I slept in the night before? Who had dressed me at the orphanage? What had I eaten that morning? Was I scared when they took me out of the room I'd lived in for almost a year, and into the big wide world?

I know almost nothing about my life up until the second it joined with theirs.

If we go to the orphanage today, I thought to myself, I'll take a lot of pictures. Not just for me, but so that little Phoenix can fill in some of those blanks for herself, right from the start.

But we didn't get to visit the orphanage that day. We didn't get to go there at all.

Mom made some calls using the phone in the lobby. With the hotel receptionist as translator, she spoke to someone at the orphanage, then to a man in a central office in Beijing. Finally, she put down the phone and turned to me.

"Apparently we were supposed to apply for permission," she said, "weeks ago. They were polite, but the message was clear. You can't do this sort of thing with a day's notice. It isn't proper protocol."

I could tell Mom was frustrated, and I was kind of touched that she was working so hard to do this for me, so I tried not to show how disappointed I was.

While we were making our calls, the couples from Clare's travel group began to gather in the restaurant. Some of them carried diaper bags and held official-looking papers under their arms. Each couple paused by the windows, not admiring the view this time but peering down toward the road. They all looked nervous and excited as they gathered to wait for their daughters.

There was no sign of Clare.

I told Mom, "Those couples are adopting babies today. From my orphanage."

I thought she'd be surprised but she wasn't.

Mom said, "When Auntie Lou suggested the trip to China, I went to our agency's website and discovered that their next adoption group was coming out here. The time-line coincided with your March Break. So I bought our tickets as part of the group. It's less expensive that way. We'll have to leave before they do, though. There's only time for us to stay in Yangshuo for three days, but they will be here longer than that to finalize the adoptions."

I would have liked to stick around the hotel and see the babies arrive, but Mom said we had so little time to see everything, and the babies could be hours late. We had a quick breakfast, then packed our day bags. I was still carrying around with me two very big secrets: things I didn't want Mom to find if she went snooping through my stuff. The posters Raizel had made—how could I ever explain those to Mom?—and my dad's wedding ring, still in its little black box.

I put my wallet on top and zipped up my backpack, then Mom and I headed out to see the sights.

First, we took a bamboo raft along the Li River, which was long, muddy, and winding. A light mist rose off the water, stinking of rotten fish. Our guide pushed us through it with his long pole, as if the mist was thick as syrup. He had dark brown arms, tough as leather from years of working outdoors. The rafting was okay for a bit, and the scenery was kind of spectacular but, after an hour or so, I felt like an old person. It might have been better if it was a speedboat or something.

Next, we watched some fishermen demonstrate how they use trained cormorants to catch fish. Mom said the locals had been catching fish this way along the Li River for hundreds of years. Every fisherman tied a rope around his cormorant's neck before the bird dived. That was so the cormorant couldn't gobble up the fish he caught. One by one, each bird surfaced with a fish in its beak, hopped onto its master's bamboo raft, and dropped the fish at his feet. Raizel would have sniffed and said that none of it was very authentic, because some of the fishermen even had cell phones—I saw one of them using his. Plus, these days, they only do the traditional sort of fishing to impress tourists. But it was still neat.

There were no wild cormorants on the water, though. Only the ones the fishermen had reared.

All the time, right through the morning, I couldn't stop thinking about Clare. Again and again I wondered: does she have her daughter by now? Is little Phoenix with her mom?

After the cormorants, we had a big meal in a famous Italian restaurant. It felt weird and kind of wrong, eating pizza in the middle of China, on a terrace that played Italian music but looked out over Karst peaks and traditional Chinese houses. We still did it, though, and the pizza tasted amazing.

When we left the restaurant, Mom found us a taxi. We climbed in the back and she pulled a piece of paper from her pocket. It was a faded photocopy with some Chinese characters on it. Mom leaned forward and spoke to the driver.

"*Xing fu cun,*" she said, hesitantly. She had the paper ready to show him, but he didn't need it.

Xing fu cun. I had heard those words before. *Xing fu* was the name of the place where I had been found.

We drove along a road that followed the banks of the river. We passed tourists riding bikes or on foot, and lots of tuk tuks, which were motorcycles with little covered benches on the back for people to sit on. It looked like a pretty cool way to get around. Then our driver made a sudden turn onto a road that wasn't paved at all, and we wound upward between the pointy hills. We didn't see any tourists up there. Just farmers, now and then, with tools slung over their shoulders. Once, we passed a strong man about my dad's age, walking beside a water buffalo. On its back was a little girl. She rode with one hand on the animal's neck and another on her father's shoulder. Maybe it was the bumpy ride or maybe it was something else, but the girl was laughing so loudly we could hear her clearly as we drove past. I twisted around and looked through the back window, watching that girl for as long as I could. Is this what my China life might have been like, if I'd had a chance to live it? Would I sometimes have ridden a water buffalo through spring sunshine while my dad—brown and strong—flicked lazily at its rear with a whip?

But that kid on the water buffalo was a lot younger than me. If I'd grown up in China, where would I be now? In school, studying hard so I could one day have a better life? Working long hours in a factory somewhere? Married, even?

We passed through several villages, one after the other. Some of them were no more than a few tiny houses clinging to the hillside. As we drove through one of the villages, an old woman stepped out in front of our taxi. She carried a string bag filled with pomelos. I knew what they were because pomelos are my mom's favorite fruit, and she always buys one whenever we go to Chinatown. But Mom didn't have any interest in buying one today. She shook her head impatiently and the taxi drove on.

Moments later, our cab drove slowly into a village that looked no different from all the others. Miniature one-story houses crammed up against each other along both sides of the main street. Here and there, narrow unpaved alleys snaked away into shadow. All the houses were made of identical gray stone. They had tattered red lanterns strung between them, and red and gold pictures of emperors or gods or something on each side of their doors. Beyond the village, up a slope, I could see a patchwork of muddy fields and, in each field, tiny figures that worked the dirt with nothing but hand tools and maybe a water buffalo.

Our taxi came to a stop along the main street, joining a line of other taxis, all waiting for customers. This kind of surprised me because you wouldn't expect tourists to come up here. Was Xing fu famous for something?

We got out of the cab. I moved to stand close to Mom and we looked around. I could smell meat cooking, and roasted garlic. I could taste the dust of the road in my mouth.

It was late afternoon and the village was quiet, but it certainly wasn't deserted. All along the main road we saw old women sitting in sunshine, small baskets of fruits and vegetables spread out in front of them to sell. Little children chased each other in and out of their homes. We heard rapid chatter and laughter from inside the houses. In an open doorway, a girl about my age sat on a low stool, mending a fishing net that she had spread out around her feet.

"This is it," Mom said.

The village where my birth parents lived.

The village where I was born.

We walked slowly down the road and, although no one passed us, I had the feeling that we were being watched from the inside of all the houses. Did the people wonder why we were there? At one point, a small boy raced out of an alley, chasing a half-deflated ball. It stopped with a thud at my feet and he dove to get it. When he looked up, our eyes met for a second, then he was gone.

We turned into another street. Outside all the houses were trestle tables. The people had been selling something, maybe to tourists who used the taxis we had seen, but it was late in the afternoon, and whatever they had been selling was mostly packed away.

"A lot of artists live in this village," Mom said. "I read that somewhere online."

Why would anyone have taken the time to write anything about this place? It was even smaller and poorer than I'd imagined. A collection of dirty old houses crumbling away on the side of a hill and not much more. I don't know exactly what I'd expected, but it wasn't this. Part of me wanted to take hold of Mom's hand and not let go. Maybe I was scared of losing myself, now I was finally here in the village where I had been born. Standing in this broken-down old place, I had the feeling I no longer knew who I was.

After a short walk, we came to a high wooden gate set into a long brick wall. From inside the gate came the sound of singing. A child's voice, trilling a few notes then pausing as if for approval, and repeating the song again and then again.

I thought it sounded beautiful, but someone was coaching her and it was easy to tell they weren't so pleased. The voice grew tenser and more strained each time the child repeated her song. I could tell she was trying to be strong, but it was getting harder and she might break down in tears at any moment. I felt sorry for her. I wanted to shout that the song was lovely, and to make her love it herself.

Mom paused at the wooden gate and looked down at the place where wood met the dirt of the road. "The gates of Xing fu school," she said. "According to the paperwork from your orphanage, you were found right here. Wrapped up in a shawl."

I didn't know what to say. Didn't know what to think. Just looked down at the dirt, as if there might still be the imprint of a baby's shape, right there in the dust. Mom slid an arm around my shoulder. She pulled me toward her and, without really intending to, I leaned my cheek on her arm.

It was a long time before either of us spoke.

There were no words.

At last, Mom said in an almost-whisper, "I'm betting you have my cell phone in your backpack. Why don't I use it to take a photo for you?"

I shrugged. I didn't need a photograph. This wasn't a place I was ever going to forget.

I stared at the spot where wood met dirt. At the narrow strip of earth where a baby might have been safe from passing cars or bikes. A picture came into my mind. It was my birth mother, young and sad, creeping through the night with me cuddled up against her for the last time. Placing me gently in the dirt, wrapped in a shawl to keep me warm because that was the only thing left she could do for me. Creeping off into the shadows with an aching in her empty arms. Had she cried? I would have cried. My heart would have broken apart to do something like that. To not have any other options left.

And all the time we stood there, the girl's song went on and on inside the school gates, becoming more strained and desperate each time she sang it.

"Mom," I said, "please, can we go back to the hotel now?"

I needed to see all those babies, waiting back at the Li River Inn, safe in the arms of people who would love them.

We headed back to the line of taxis, which was shorter now that most of the tourists had left for the day. All the way along the windy mud road down to the Li River, we sat in silence. At one point, I stopped wallowing in my own feelings long enough to wonder if this was a tough day for Mom, too. Picturing the little baby who became her daughter, lying in the street all alone. As the cab pulled up outside the hotel,

Mom said, “We try to empathize with other people, Kelly, but we can never truly know what they face in their lives. We can’t know how others struggle, and why they make the decisions they do.”

She was probably talking about my birth parents. But what she said was true of my dad, too, and maybe also true of Mom.

She paid the driver and we went inside.

For the last few hours, since we’d arrived in the village where I was born, I hadn’t thought much about Clare and baby Phoenix. But now I did. I wanted to see them both. To see some happiness. I wondered if Clare would be sitting at the table where we’d chatted last night, but this time with a wriggling baby in her arms.

Maybe Mom was wondering about the babies, too, because she followed me into the restaurant. At first it seemed deserted, especially because it was so silent in there, but then we began to see them. A couple by the far wall, side by side and so close together that you couldn’t even tell which knee their new baby was sitting on. The mom and dad were smiling at each other and at her. Lost in a happiness that turned the rest of the world into something distant and unimportant. The baby’s eyes were red and swollen, showing how she had struggled through the changes of the last few hours, but she wasn’t crying anymore. She had already taken a step away from her old world and into her new one. Her dad was feeding her Cheerios from a plastic container, and she was figuring out how to take them in her fat little fist and transfer them into her mouth. It was a new skill, and her parents were smiling so proudly because they were the first ones to see it. They had only been together for a few hours, these three people, but you could tell that already they were a family.

There were two other new families in the restaurant as well. One stood by the railing, looking out over the hills. Their daughter was asleep in her mom's arms. Another couple was trying to eat dinner. Their baby was still struggling, still fighting against all the new changes in her life. She was being held by her dad and, each time he looked at her, she arched her back and turned away.

"It's so hard for some of them at first," Mom said. "I wish you could see them all a week from now. It doesn't take long for the babies to adjust. They'll be thriving in a few days."

Clare was nowhere to be seen.

Perhaps she was in her room, bonding with Phoenix. Maybe showing her a photo of the dad she would never know.

Thinking about this made me miss my own dad so much. "I wish Dad could be here with us," I told Mom.

Mom rested a hand on my shoulder. "Your father wishes he could share this with you," Mom said. "I'm sure he thinks about you all the time."

We stood together, watching the babies for a few more minutes. Then Mom yawned.

"I'm wiped," she said. "It might be time for an early night." She turned and went up to our room.

But something bothered me. Something that had nothing to do with all the emotional events of the day. I felt troubled and I couldn't put my finger on why.

When I feel sad and confused at home, what I like to do is chat on Facebook with Raizel. There was a computer in the lobby, so I paid some money to the man at the front desk and he gave me a code. Minutes later I was online.

But there was no Facebook. Maybe it was blocked or something. Suddenly, Raizel and my life back home felt very far away.

I leaned back on the chair and tried to figure out what was bothering me so much. Why did I feel upset? It hadn't started, this feeling, until just before Mom left to lie down. What was it she had said, before leaving?

Your father wishes he could share this with you.

How could Mom know that? Neither of us had a clue where Dad was, and the only way he would even know about this trip was if my postcard had reached him. Dad had driven to Loblaws one morning months ago and never returned. Neither of us had the faintest clue why. Every time I'd asked Mom how we could get in touch with Dad, she had shaken her head sadly and said that she had no idea.

Your father wishes he could share this with you.

Had she meant to say this? Did she even realize she had said it?

That's when it hit me.

What if Mom had known all along where Dad was? What if she knew all about Dad moving to Vancouver, and how to get in touch with him, and she'd kept those things a secret, just like China, and selling the swords, and moving us in with Auntie Lou?

What if Mom was the reason I hadn't been able to speak to Dad all these months?

It seemed too horrible to believe. Mom might have her secrets, but would she really keep my dad from me? The longer I thought about them, though, the stranger her words seemed. And the more cold and shivery I became.

Mom would need a way to contact Dad if she wanted to sell the house. She'd have to know where he was for a whole bunch of practical reasons.

It was terrifying. Despite all her lies and secrets, I couldn't believe my mom would be capable of something like this.

There was one way to find out for sure.

I glanced at the stairway leading up to our room, then turned back to the computer and signed into Mom's gmail account. This was the second time. When I'd done it at the library, I'd felt really bad for snooping, but this time I didn't feel bad at all.

I needed to know.

I typed in Mom's password. A few seconds and I was in.

I scrolled through her emails. There were lots from Auntie Lou, as well as tons of junk, and emails from the adoption agency about our trip. Two messages from Raizel's mom, and one from the company that bought Dad's swords.

I kept on scrolling down and, on the third page, I found them.

Three emails from my dad.

There were even more, further on. Emails going back weeks and weeks, all of them sent from an address I didn't know.

I started to read. The messages were blunt and business-like. Not the sort of emails you would write to your wife. They were mostly about bills and stuff like that. But in one email, Dad talked about himself. An audition he had done for a theater company in Vancouver. The condo he was buying. The British pub at the end of his road.

Not a single one of Dad's emails mentioned me. He didn't ask how I was, or if I missed him, or anything. It was like I didn't exist for him at all.

Feeling numb, I scrolled through Mom's emails to Dad. There were even more of those. She told him about the headaches, and Auntie Lou helping us out, and how she was going to sell his swords. Her messages were as formal-sounding as his. Boring things, like taxes and what to do with our old car. She mentioned that we'd spent Christmas day with Auntie Lou, but she didn't say that, for me, it had been the most miserable Christmas of my life, I missed Dad so much. In fact, just like Dad, Mom barely mentioned me.

So many emails stretching back for months, right up to the week after Dad had left to buy milk and had walked himself out of my life.

If Mom knew where Dad was and how I could reach him, why hadn't she said?

This was one secret too much.

I clicked *New Message* and sent a note to Mom. All it said was: *WHY DID YOU KEEP MY DAD FROM ME?* No subject heading and no name at the end. I imagined Mom reading the note, puzzling over it, then going cold all over as the truth dawned.

If it hurt her, I didn't care. After what she had done, she deserved to be hurt.

In an early email, I found Dad's phone number. It had a Vancouver code. I swiped a pen from reception and wrote the number on the back of my hand.

Mom's cell phone was in my backpack, like it always was. I didn't care about the charges. I didn't care that it was probably the middle of the night in Vancouver. I just wanted to speak to my dad because now I could. What was I going to say, though? Would I tell him how hurt I felt that he had been gone for weeks and not made any effort to get in touch? That I missed him so much it was like a pain inside me all the time? Or would I just beg him to meet my flight in Vancouver? I had no clue.

I dialed the number, then let it ring and ring.

At last, someone picked up. "Daddy," I blurted out. "Dad. It's me. It's Kelly."

Silence.

"Dad?"

More silence, then the sound of a woman laughing sleepily, somewhere in the background. A voice, whispering my dad's name.

"Dad? Are you there? Please say something."

I could hear breathing. Was it his breathing? I couldn't tell.

A few more seconds, then the line went dead.

I left the hotel and started to walk. Down to the Li River,

where the sunset was already turning the water a deep red-brown, like blood. There was a pathway that ran along the banks of the river, out of the hotel gardens and beyond. I took the path, and just walked and walked.

After a while, I passed two old fishermen. It was the end of a busy day for them, and they stood ankle deep in the muddy water, talking and laughing. I paused to watch them for a bit. They were just being happy together in a place where they belonged. Like it was something they always did when they finished work. Where did I belong? With Mom, who lied and kept me from my dad? With Dad, who was content to live a life that didn't have me in it? Or here in China? This country wasn't alive. I hadn't seen a single wild bird anywhere the entire time we had been here. Not in Beijing and not in Yangshuo. It was just like Jade had said.

I left the old men behind and walked on and on.

I thought of the babies, crying for their lost lives inside the hotel. Clare, grieving for her husband, who had died even before he got to meet his daughter. I thought of my Finding Place and the dozens of sad bundles that must have been set down in front of those gates over years and years. So many bundles, and mine just one of them.

I felt as if I'd become that little lost bundle all over again.

By the time I stopped walking, the river was completely black, except for the reflection of a perfect round moon as it swam slowly downstream.

Night had fallen and I was a long way from the hotel.

I sat down, my back against a thick stem of bamboo. For a while I looked at the river, just thinking, then I opened my backpack and pulled out Raizel's package of posters. I tilted the top one toward the moonlight so I could look at it more closely. Raizel had always been kind of obsessed about the birth-parent thing, treating it like a fun mystery that needed solving. But that had never made much sense to me. Why would I even want to find my birth parents? It had seemed like a weird and crazy idea when she brought it up. But somehow, it didn't seem so crazy anymore.

I sat for hours and hours beside that river, under fronds of bamboo that shook like fists. The sky blackened and stars blinked in the water. When the wind stroked its surface, the stars exploded like fireworks then settled back into being stars again. The fronds shivered, the river lapped against the bank and, ever so slowly, the anger went away.

Maybe that's when I would have walked back. Gone up to our hotel room and slipped into bed. I think this is what could have happened, but it didn't. Because sitting there by the river, feeling sad and exhausted by all the emotions of the day, I fell asleep.

While I slept, the moon traveled all the way across the sky, then disappeared. And when I woke, the sun was rising between two of the Karst peaks. I was shivering and wet to the skin with morning dew but, for a moment, I didn't move. Didn't open my eyes. Something was different. I struggled to remember where I was and to figure out what had changed. Why I felt so wonderful, even though I was wet all over.

And then, the instant before my eyes opened, I knew.

It was birdsong.

My eyes snapped open and I looked out onto the river.

Wild birds. Hundreds and hundreds of them.

Cormorants, like ballerinas all in black. Ducks squabbling on the banks. Waders picking through the shallows. Herons winging overhead, their outlines blurred by morning mist and their feathers tinted pink by the sun.

Birds as still as statues.

Birds floating calmly downstream.

Birds singing in the new day.

Maybe more birds than I'd ever seen in one place for my whole entire life.

Jade was wrong.

I knew for sure now.

She was wrong.

5

鸟儿

BIRDS

The herons on Lesley Street Spit had always been special to me, but they were nothing compared to what I was seeing now. This was a dream wrapped up in mist. A secret glimpse of a world that was totally wild and magical.

I held my breath, willing my body to stay still even though I was cold and wet and stiff. The birds didn't know that I was there. I didn't want to disturb them. I didn't want to intrude.

Seconds stretched into minutes. I had the feeling of being part of something that would stay with me my whole entire life. Connected in a deeper way than I'd ever been connected to anything, either in Canada or in China.

Then something spooked them.

A thousand wings pulsed and the birds on the water rose together, climbing into the sky. On the bank beside me, the ducks flapped, panicked, and slipped into the river.

Within the space of a few breaths, the birds were gone as if they had never existed. The river was silent and still, waiting for the sun to warm it. The whole thing could have been no more than a dream.

Except it wasn't a dream. It was real. All of it.

I stood up and stretched. This was the first time I'd ever slept outside. The first time I'd ever been on my own for an entire night. The thought was kind of exhilarating.

The more awake I became, though, the more my troubles came back. I thought about Dad. Why hadn't he even asked Mom how I was? Why did he put the phone down without a word? And who was the laughing woman? I'd kind of assumed that when I got to Vancouver airport, Dad would be there to welcome me. But what if he didn't want me anymore?

Then there was my mom.

Did she even care that I was gone? Was she frantic with worry or just relieved? Mom had told me a lot of lies, and she had kept my dad from me for months and months. Maybe that meant she didn't love me anymore, either.

If both my parents could betray me like this, then what was left?

Whether or not she cared, Mom was still going to be mad at me when I got back. Really mad, because she had told me not to go off by myself, and I had disappeared for the whole entire night. Likely she would ground me for the rest of the trip. I would die if she did something like that.

But it wasn't too late. There was a good chance Mom

hadn't figured out yet that I was missing. Most likely, she had gone straight to bed and fallen asleep. Unless she'd wakened during the night, she probably didn't know that I wasn't in the hotel. If I was quick, I could head back, sneak into our room, and Mom would never have to know that I had left.

On the top of a ridge that ran alongside the river was the road we had driven on the day before. Early morning sunshine was already hitting the road, so I decided to walk back to the hotel that way, so my clothes would dry out. I took one last look at the river, but not a single bird remained. Then I climbed up to the road and started the long walk back.

I had only been walking maybe five minutes or so when a taxi drove by. The driver stopped a little ahead of me and waited until I caught up, then he opened the window and shouted something I couldn't understand. It was obvious what he meant, though. He was asking if I needed a ride. There was money in my backpack and I was cold and wet, so I nodded and climbed in. The driver leaned over his shoulder to look at me, waiting for me to tell him where to go. I opened my mouth to say "Li River Inn," but something quite different came out.

"Xing fu cun. Xie xie."

The taxi turned around in the road and sped off, away from our hotel, back the way I had walked, up the windy unpaved road between the Karst peaks, and toward the village where I had been born.

My heart was beating so fast I thought the driver would hear it. He glanced at me through the mirror, then turned the heating up full so my clothes would dry. Looking concerned, he asked why I was going to Xing fu cun. Family, I told him. My family is there. He nodded, satisfied.

It was half the truth, anyway.

This was something I needed to do quickly, before the anger faded. Before I thought things through and admitted to myself what a bad idea it was.

I opened Raizel's package and read through the English translation of Miss Wu's posters for the hundredth time:

Found, outside the village school, June 16th, 2001, age one day:

Baby Girl.

If I am your daughter, please call me.

I would like to meet you.

Contact me here: ______________________________

Kelly Mei Stroud.

I wondered which contact number to put on the posters. Using Mom's cell number felt a bit weird because she had no idea this was even happening. And anyway, would my birth parents want to call an international number?

In the bottom of my backpack was a flier for the Li River Inn. I copied their telephone number neatly onto each of the posters, underneath Miss Wu's beautiful Chinese calligraphy. There was no scotch tape in my backpack and no push pins, of course, but Mom had given me our small first aid kit to carry and there were a lot of Band-Aids inside. So that's what I would use instead.

The driver stopped at the end of the line of taxis, just like the day before. There were only two other taxis in line but as we stopped, another one pulled up behind us and a Chinese couple got out, cameras slung around their necks. Tourists were beginning to arrive. I felt pretty sure there would be a taxi here for me to take, once I was done.

I put up every single one of the posters. On the front walls of the houses, all the way along the main street. On shop windows and fences. Doorways and tourist signs. I even went back to my Finding Place—though it was just as hard to see it for the second time—and stuck a poster to the brick wall right beside the gate.

Each poster I hung made me feel just a little bit better, connected to the village where I'd been born, as if I could finally see that, even though Canada had been my world for more than twelve years, here was somewhere else I belonged.

As the stack of papers dwindled in my hands, the village came to life around me. People left their homes to start the day, some of them pausing in front of my posters to discuss them even before I'd moved out of sight. While I watched from the corner, one young woman with a baby on her hip read my poster with her finger moving underneath each character. As she did so, she shook her head slowly from side to side. I wondered if it was me she disapproved of or my birth mother.

Standing across the road from the school, I watched as the gates opened and children in smart green uniforms filed inside to start their day. Some of the older ones paused briefly to read my poster, chattering to each other. One of the last children to enter was a small boy, several years younger than me. He glanced around him, then tore the poster from the wall and crumpled it into his pocket. I peered at his hair, trying to see if it was jet black, or a chestnut brown with auburn highlights where the sunlight struck it. But he was too far away for me to tell.

I had none of the posters left now. The school bell rang, and the voices from the other side of the wall fell silent. The village had begun its day and, for everyone here except me, it was a day like any other. A truck picked up about twenty men, all of them dressed in work clothes, and disappeared down the road. Neighbors gathered in the street to chat. People moved into their routines as if they were part of a dance that got repeated over and over, and I stood in the middle of it all, silent and invisible.

It was a beautiful morning and the sun shone warm on my cheeks. Now I was here, what difference would another few minutes make? I decided to explore.

Strolling down one alley and up another, I tried not to look like I was peeking in the windows. I wanted to blend in, though you can't really do that when you're a stranger in a small village. Not even if you look like everyone else.

On a narrow street behind the school, an old man sat on a stool outside his house. There was a stained trestle table in front of him. On the table he had placed a piece of paper and a plate filled with ink. I paused to watch as he dipped the side of his hand into the ink, then made a mark on the paper. He dipped again, and once more his hand danced.

In front of my eyes, a scene was taking shape. A painting of the Karst peaks. The Li River. A cormorant in the foreground and, in its beak, a fish.

"That's so great!" I said in English without really thinking, stunned at what he could do in a few seconds without even a brush—just ink and the side of his own hand. The artist looked up, startled. He hadn't realized I was there. Quickly, I translated the words in my mind.

"*Ni hua de fei chang hao*," I said.

The artist smiled.

A pretty girl hurried out of the house behind him. She was carrying red silk cloths, dusty and worn from long use, which she spread on the ground at his feet. She returned to the house, then emerged again with dozens of similar paintings, which she displayed on the cloth.

"For the tourists," the artist told me, speaking slowly in Chinese. "Today there will be tourists from Guilin."

I realized he had figured out my Chinese wasn't good, and he was choosing simple words so I would understand. I smiled and nodded. Then I surprised myself. "Could you teach me?" I asked in halting Mandarin. "Could I learn to do this?"

The man glanced down toward the road, perhaps wondering how long he had before the tourists arrived. Then he stood up, patted the seat, and said, "Please, sit down."

He gave me a blank piece of paper. I dipped the side of my hand in ink, and he showed me how to make different kinds of marks on the paper by twisting my wrist. He demonstrated what a palm print could do, and the effects that were possible with the end of a finger or the edge of a nail. I thought of Raizel and how many afternoons we had spent, teaching ourselves to draw Manga. I wished she could see me now. This was so amazing.

When I looked up, it wasn't only the artist who was watching me. The pretty girl was watching, too, as well as a man in a white apron who had walked over from the house next door. All three of them were smiling down at me.

"You will be very good at this," said the artist.

I thought carefully, forming Chinese phrases in my mind. "My mom is an artist," I told him hesitantly. "She gave me her skill."

After I said that, I wondered if it really was true. Did I get my art talent from my mom or my birth parents? Could you get a talent from an adopted parent, or did it come from your genes? I had no idea, but I knew that when I first started to draw, it was because I wanted to be just like my mom.

Thinking about Mom made me wonder whether she had missed me yet. Was she worried enough now that I'd be able to tell in her eyes how much I still mattered to her? Or was she beyond that—so worried she had called the police?

When that possibility occurred to me, I started to panic.

"Thank you," I told the man in Chinese. "Now I have to go."

By the time the taxi dropped me off outside the Li River Inn, it was the middle of the morning. What had happened in the time I had been gone? Would I find police in the lobby? Locals volunteering for a search party? People searching the river, thinking maybe I had fallen in and drowned?

I had wanted to worry Mom, yes, but I hadn't wanted to cause trouble.

I paid the driver and ran inside.

In the lobby everything was calm, as if nothing had happened. Two people stood by the door with a huge pile of suitcases. A small boy was playing a game on the computer, and the desk clerk was chatting with someone over the phone.

As the receptionist finished her call, I stepped forward and gave her my name, expecting some sort of reaction. There was no recognition on her face. Trying to sound casual, I asked if anyone had been looking for me. She shook her head, puzzled.

Maybe Mom knew I was missing and she had chosen not to tell anyone. Was she truly relieved to have me gone?

I turned away from the front desk and toward the stairs that led up to our room. The couple with the suitcases had gone, but someone else was there. One person, standing by the window, looking out at the peaks. And that person was Clare.

Just Clare. No baby.

Where was Phoenix?

"Clare?"

I was so frightened of what she might tell me that I almost didn't ask. But I had to find out what had happened. Every other couple had their baby. Where was hers?

Clare turned around when she heard me call her name. Her eyes were bloodshot and swollen. "Oh ... it's you," she said. She seemed relieved to see me.

"Where's your baby?"

The question was kind of blunt, but Clare didn't seem to care.

"Yesterday morning," she said, "they came from the orphanage. All the nannies and everyone else's baby. But they didn't bring Phoenix."

I peered at Clare's face, but it was hard to read what she was feeling. Maybe she'd learned how to hide things. It was something I wished I knew how to do.

"The orphanage director took me aside. He used a translator to tell me that my baby had been very sick. She had lost a lot of weight. There were things she could do before her illness that she didn't seem able to do anymore, such as sitting up by herself. They told me I should wait here for a few days and perhaps find out if another baby could be referred. But how could I just choose a different baby? This baby is my daughter. I've already started to love her."

Clare didn't have a sad-happy smile anymore. She didn't have any smile at all.

"My parents said they fell in love with me on the day they first saw my referral photos," I told her.

"Exactly," Clare replied. "I wanted to scream at them when they suggested I should take another baby. As if my daughter could be switched with someone else's and it wouldn't make any difference." Clare folded her arms and squeezed herself. It was like she was cuddling the empty space where her baby should have been. "I wanted to tell them to bring me Phoenix no matter how sick she was. But then I stopped to think. I'll be raising this child alone. No husband. Not even family nearby. With a healthy child, that would be tough enough, but a daughter with health problems? Perhaps this baby would be better off with someone other than me."

I dropped my backpack on the floor and moved closer.

"What did you do?" I asked.

Please. Don't tell me you gave up on her.

"I asked to go back to the orphanage with the nannies, so I could see her. I thought that would help me make a decision."

"And did it?"

Clare sighed. "She was so ... limp. The baby who was supposed to be Phoenix. She's nearly eleven months old but she looked so tiny and frail. I wanted to bring her with me right there and then and care for her. But they wouldn't let me. They said I should think about it seriously overnight. Consider what it might mean if the illness had left her with permanent damage. They said, 'Tell us your answer tomorrow.' But no one's even sure what's wrong with her. How can I know whether I'll be able to cope when the doctors can't even say for sure what's wrong?"

Clare was holding the little embroidered pouch that had her referral photos inside. I wondered if she had been looking at them all morning. Even as we talked, she turned the little purse over and over in her hands.

I felt so sad for her. But I felt even sorrier for the little girl who was supposed to be Phoenix. Left alone in her room in the orphanage, all the other babies adopted and gone away. If she didn't get to be Clare's daughter, how long would she have to wait for a family? Maybe she would grow up in the orphanage, never having a home of her own.

Clare said, "What should I do?" I hoped she was wondering out loud and not really asking me, because I didn't know anything about raising a kid, healthy or sick. I'd only been one of those kids. But at least that was something to share.

I said, "A few weeks before Mom and Dad came to China to get me, a woman got in touch with them. She had just adopted a baby from the orphanage where I was living. She told my dad she had seen me, and I was small and very sick." I had heard this story so many times that I could play the conversation word for word in my head. "Mom and Dad could have changed their minds about adopting me after that, but they didn't. They came out to China for me, just as they had planned. And I was perfectly fine. Maybe if they had listened to that lady, then I would have grown up in the orphanage, and someone else would have got to be me."

Clare said, "But there's no guarantee the same will happen with Phoenix. I've seen her and she doesn't look fine at all."

I thought of the baby girl whose future hung in the balance. I was desperate to help her.

I took a deep breath.

"Can I ... er ... ask you a difficult question?"

Clare nodded.

"It's kind of personal."

She hesitated, then nodded again.

"If you had been pregnant when the car accident happened, and they said your baby might have been damaged inside of you, what would you have done?"

Clare looked shocked. "What do you mean?" she asked.

I know this was cruel of me, but all I could think about was little Phoenix and how she might lose her chance of ever having a family.

"I mean, would you have had an abortion? If you were pregnant, would you have got rid of the baby?"

"No! Of course not!"

I looked calmly at her. "This is the same thing," I said. "Phoenix is yours, just like a baby inside your body. Isn't she?"

Clare didn't answer.

There was nothing else I could do. I turned toward the stairs, leaving her alone by the window, looking out at the funny mountains and struggling with maybe the toughest decision of her life.

I paused outside our hotel room, one hand resting on the door. I didn't want to go inside. If Mom had hoped I wouldn't ever come back, then I was going to see it in her eyes. And if she had been frantic with worry, then I knew what would happen. Total relief, then anger.

There was no doubt about it. Mom was going to ground me after this.

I opened the door.

Mom was sitting on her bed. She was still wearing her pajamas even though it was nearly time for lunch. She had a blanket wrapped around her shoulders and she was slumped forward like an old person, watching TV with the sound on mute.

"Hello."

Her voice sounded deadened. Not disappointed I was back, and not relieved or angry. Just totally blank. Her face showed no emotion, either. It was very weird and kind of worrying. She looked past me, not directly at me, when she spoke.

"I'm so sorry ... sweetie." The words came out slowly. I had the strangest feeling that she was calling me sweetie because she couldn't remember my name.

"Mom?"

"This headache was very bad. I woke up late and then ... it started. You had already gone downstairs. It was ... I couldn't even see properly. It's taken ... a long time for it to go away."

Mom massaged her temples. She let the blanket slip from her shoulders, then shuffled into the bathroom. I heard her turn on the shower. After that, she appeared in the doorway again.

"Are ... are you okay?" I asked her.

"No," she said, "I'm not okay. I feel guilty for wasting our time when we have so little of it. I'm sorry, darling."

Mom went back into the bathroom and closed the door.

I know it sounds horrible with Mom feeling so ill, but I was totally relieved. All the crazy things I'd done—running away, staying out all night—and somehow I'd gotten away with it. Mom had been asleep, then stuck in the room with a headache, and she didn't even know I'd been gone. Everything was just the way it had been the day before, except that I'd found out about another one of Mom's secrets. And in a small village up in the hills, everyone likely knew by now that a baby who had lived among them for just a day was trying to find out where she belonged.

While Mom was showering, I slipped out of my muddy clothes and ran a brush through my hair. The person I saw in the mirror looked different in a way that was hard to explain. Younger and older at the same time. And definitely more Chinese.

"You should have woken me before you went down," Mom shouted from the shower. "How was breakfast? Did you go for a walk?"

I tossed my backpack on one of the crumpled beds and glanced at the TV. A bunch of soap opera stars were playing out their pretend lives, probably shouting at each other, though the flick of a mute switch had taken away their power.

"A stupid headache and we've lost a whole morning."

"You don't need to worry, Mom," I shouted in reply. Mom cared about me. Otherwise, why would she even have brought me back to China? I was her daughter, so it couldn't be easy to face the fact that I also belonged somewhere else.

Maybe if Mom hadn't brought me back to China, I would have grown up thinking Jade was right: that China was a country so messed up it didn't even have any wild birds left. I thought about what I'd seen that morning. So many hundreds of birds, floating down the river in a pink mist.

Mom turned off the shower. "Kelly?" she shouted. "Are you still there?"

"I'm still here, Mom," I yelled back. "I'm here. Don't worry. Everything will be okay."

6

危机

CRISIS

But everything wasn't okay. It hadn't been okay for a very long time.

For just one day, things seemed better: our last day in Yangshuo. But I had seen all those emails from Dad, and you can't un-see something like that. You also can't easily forgive someone who takes your dad from you. So things may have seemed all right for a while, but everything was bound to blow up, sooner or later.

It wasn't until we reached Beijing that things fell apart, our lives completely unraveling in one long afternoon and one very long night.

On the plane to Beijing I couldn't stop wondering what Clare had done about her baby. Had she gone back for Phoenix? I had wanted so badly to see her again before we left but, even though I kept hanging around in the foyer and in the restaurant, there was no sign of her. Now we would probably never find out what she had chosen to do. Never see her again. By the time Clare's travel group returned to Beijing, we would be back in Canada, and I hadn't even asked for her address.

My thoughts kept drifting to my birth parents, too. Had they seen the posters yet? If so, why hadn't they been in touch? For more than twenty-four hours, they could have reached me at the Li River Inn. But now we were moving on, and what little chance I had of ever meeting them or finding out who they were, was gone. This made me sad—but also kind of relieved. Mom would be shocked and hurt if she knew what I'd done. Maybe if I had confided in her and we'd put the posters up together, she might have been okay with it, but I'd done everything behind her back. And the more I stopped to think about it, the less sure I was that finding my birth parents was even something I wanted. What if they turned out to be bad people? Then I'd have to spend the rest of my life worrying there could be something bad inside of me.

Finding your birth parents was something you needed to think through carefully. And I hadn't taken time to think about it at all.

It was the middle of the afternoon when we arrived back in our Beijing hotel. We'd only been away three days, but so much had happened that it felt like forever. We were both ravenous. We hauled our suitcases into the room, then headed straight down to the hotel restaurant to get food.

It was closed.

"Too late for lunch," Mom said, "and too early for dinner." She glanced over to the revolving doors. "I suppose we could get a cab somewhere."

"No need, Mom."

I told her about the road I'd found nearby where there was a whole strip of little restaurants and cafes, all with red lanterns hanging outside. One of them was bound to be open.

And it was. In fact, they all were. We chose one of the smaller restaurants because there were a lot of people eating there. Inside, it was warm, busy, and loud. They gave us a table right next to the window and brought us menus with no English on them at all. My spoken Chinese might be okay, but I knew hardly any characters. And I didn't feel like speaking Chinese to the waiter, especially not in front of Mom. So we peered around at other people's food to find something we each thought we might like to eat, then pointed, to show that was what we wanted. Mom chose a slimy looking rice dish with lots of shellfish sticking out of it. I chose tofu with bok choy. Then we sat back down.

"Well, that was a bit of an adventure," Mom said, smiling as the waiter left with our order. If that was an adventure, it was a pretty lame one.

The food came quickly and we shoveled it down. The tofu tasted delicious, which was good because it would be my last meal for a while, though I didn't know it then. Mom finished her meal first and, as I heaved in the last mouthful, I caught her looking at me across the table. She was leaning forward with her arms folded, suddenly serious and very intense.

"We should talk," Mom said.

I didn't say a thing. I guess I'd known this would have to happen sooner or later.

"Kelly, I know you were very upset with me when you found out about moving in with Auntie Lou. I understand it isn't something you want. The thing is, we might not have a choice. Financially, we're not doing so well."

"But—"

"What I am sorry for is the way I told you. I lost my temper and I still regret that."

I couldn't think of anything to say.

Mom continued, "If you stop to think about it, living with Auntie Lou is a good idea for lots of reasons. She has a big house and she lives all alone. Lou is the principal at a high school with a really great reputation, so it also makes sense in terms of your future. And I wouldn't have to cope on my own anymore."

"But I hate Auntie Lou," I said in a kind of whiny voice, "She's too bossy."

"That's your father talking."

"And I hate that you didn't ask what I wanted."

Mom said, "Well, we can talk some more once we're back in Canada. I have some difficult decisions to make, that's all I'm saying. Let's just wait and see what happens. Okay?"

Wait and see. Her answer to everything.

Wait and see.

"You say you have some decisions to make," I snapped,

"but what about me? We should make big decisions together. We should at least discuss things."

"You're impossible to talk to these days. Do you realize that?"

"Why can't we go on the way we are?"

Mom sighed.

"Kelly, your dad never earned much as an actor, but it was something. Now we have to survive without the money he brought in. I can't cover the mortgage. We have to sell the house because without your dad, we can't make ends meet."

Why did Mom always have to blame Dad for everything? She wanted to drag us both off to live with Auntie Lou, and suddenly that was Dad's fault, too? He had never liked Auntie Lou. There was no way he would ever want me living with her.

"You should have thought about how much you needed Dad," I said, "before you drove him away."

Mom blinked and leaned across the table.

"What did you say?"

"You were always yelling at him, Mom. Nagging all the time. If you hadn't made him want to leave, we wouldn't have to move house."

"Kelly, I didn't ..."

Mom paused in mid-sentence while the waiter topped up our tea. She gave him a strained sort of smile, said, "*Xie Xie,*" with the wrong tones, and turned back to me.

"I was not the reason your father left," she said.

I shouldn't have said any more. I should have known

when to stop. But the floodgates were open now.

"You were, Mom. You drove Dad off. All the way to Vancouver."

I crossed my arms and enjoyed the shocked look on her face. Mom's voice dropped to an almost-whisper.

"How do you know he's in Vancouver?" she asked.

I felt powerful, knowing something Mom thought she had managed to hide. So I sipped my tea a few times before answering.

"I went back to the studio," I said after a bit. "His new address was on a bit of paper taped to the door."

I reached down into my backpack and pulled out the little black box I'd found on Dad's desk at Sherwood Productions. I slid it across the table to Mom. She opened it slowly, hesitantly, as if she was scared of finding out what might be inside.

"His wedding ring," she said kind of sadly. She turned it over between her fingers as if it was a gift I'd just given her—one so precious that she was speechless.

"Mom," I said, forcing all the anger out of my voice and trying to sound as gentle as I could. "I'm not coming back to Toronto."

Mom looked up. While she had been inspecting the ring, it was as if she'd forgotten I was there.

I went on. "Before we came here, I wrote to Dad and told him I wanted to live with him. I don't know whether I was serious at the time, but I am now. I can't go live with Auntie Lou. If we have to move house, I might as well be with Dad."

I thought Mom was going to yell at me that I'd betrayed

her. I waited, but she didn't. It might have been easier if she had.

Mom gave a little cough that sounded more like a choke. She said, "What makes you think your father wants you living with him in Vancouver, Kelly?"

This was the worst thing she could have said, because it had already occurred to me. Maybe Dad had left because he didn't want me anymore.

Just then, the door burst open, making both of us jump. A big group of people—maybe students—loudly jostled their way into the restaurant, laughing and holding on to each other. The restaurant was already busy but, for a few seconds, it became so loud and chaotic that it was hard to focus on a thought, never mind a conversation. A waiter squeezed past the back of my chair, carrying a huge platter of sizzling meat and the air filled with smoke. The students struggled to find seats; several people picked up their food and shifted to different tables to make room; and in the midst of it all, somewhere in the rear of the restaurant, a baby started to wail.

Then everything calmed down a notch. I blinked smoke out of my eyes and looked at Mom again. I said softly, "You knew Dad went to Vancouver, didn't you? All this time you've known where he was, but you never said. For months, you've kept my dad from me."

I wiped a sleeve across my eyes because I didn't want Mom to think I was crying.

"I wanted to protect you," Mom said. "There were things going on in your father's life. I knew how painful it would be for you if you found out. I was trying to protect you."

The waiter came again to top up our tea, but this time Mom waved him away.

"I thought it was better for some time to pass before you had to know the truth," she said. "Now I'm thinking maybe that wasn't for the best." Mom unfastened a chain she was wearing around her neck and threaded Dad's wedding ring onto it. Then she put the chain back on and slid the ring down underneath her shirt. "Nothing like this had ever happened to me before," she said, "and it's not like I expected it ever would. You have to do the best you can. Make it up as you go along. And sometimes you make decisions that seem like good ones, only to find out later that they weren't."

She placed both her hands on the table as if to say, there are no more secrets from here on in. Then she started to talk.

"Two years ago," Mom said, "your dad started seeing someone else. She was the dancer from Sherwood Productions. Her name was Laura."

Laura.

A memory flashed through my mind. Thick gray hair, long enough to sit on. Shared secrets underneath a stage. Sunshine, and a dance I felt she was dancing for no one but me.

Mom said, "I found out about it almost right away, but I didn't say anything to him because I wanted to keep our family together at all costs. I thought that it would burn itself out. Things usually do with your dad. I thought he would come back to me. And maybe he would have. But about a year ago, your father's girlfriend got pregnant."

I gripped the edge of my seat. I didn't want to hear any more, not really. Maybe it's best sometimes not knowing things. Maybe it can even be for the best when people lie to you. But it was too late now. There was no turning back.

She went on. "It still took your dad seven months to make a decision but, when he did, he moved quickly. You know that part. He left us without warning. And now he lives in Vancouver—with his girlfriend and their baby daughter."

What do you say when someone tells you a thing like that? When you think your life has come apart as much as it can and the threads unravel even more?

There are no words.

And in that exact moment, Mom's cell phone rang.

It was in my backpack, of course. It always was. Mom and I glanced down when it started to ring. Then we looked at each other, puzzled. Neither of us was expecting a call. We didn't know anyone in China. And no one would call all the way from Canada. Not unless something was wrong.

I fished the phone out of my bag and then, because it was Mom's, and also because I didn't want to be the one to have to get bad news, I passed it to her.

Mom put the phone to her ear.

"Hello?" she said. Her eyes flicked from the table and up to me. "She is, yes. Really? They did? I see. Yes." Mom took a crumpled scrap of paper and a pen out of her pocket and scribbled down a phone number. "Thank you for passing along the message. Thank you. *Xie Xie.*"

Mom looked up from the phone. Then she laid it down on

the table. She took the slip of paper with the phone number and she pushed it across to me. I looked at it.

"A message for you," Mom said. "From your birth parents."

That was all she said for a long time.

I looked at the paper for maybe ten seconds without moving. It sat on the table in front of me like evidence. Like the first brick in a wall. I held on as long as I could. Then I reached for it. Studied it. Folded it up and placed it in the palm of my hand.

Mom said, "It seems you want to be with everyone except me. You want your dad, and you want your birth parents. Heaven knows how you managed that one. But now you have a lead. So good luck to you."

Mom had never sounded so cold and hurt before. Like a stranger. Her voice totally scared me.

I glanced toward the door.

"Are you going to walk away?" Mom asked. "Like you do every time we argue? Every time the going gets tough?"

I didn't answer but she was right. I had been thinking how I wanted to be anywhere else but here.

Mom said, "A lot of people have left us. Walked away when we needed them. From me, sure. And from you, Kelly. A lot of people. But I haven't, not once. Did you even notice that?"

She stood up and reached for her coat.

I don't know what she was planning to do. I don't know whether she would have just walked out of the restaurant and left me there. And I'll never know. Because whatever

Mom planned to do in that moment didn't have a chance to happen.

Someone was banging on the glass window. And the banging went on and on.

It wasn't the sort of thing you could ignore. We both turned around. Out on the street was a little girl. She had both hands formed into fists and she was battering the window as hard as she could, trying to get our attention. Each time her fists hit the glass, she leaped up with the effort, her legs bending and her body launching itself into the air.

"Who ..." Mom started, confused.

The little girl had a bandage on one knee.

"I know her," I told Mom.

"Well, clearly she needs to talk to you."

Mom threw a handful of notes onto the table and we headed outside.

The girl was delighted to have found me. As we left the restaurant she grabbed my arm, chattering loudly in Chinese so fast that I couldn't make out any of it.

I placed a finger over the little girl's mouth. "Slowly," I told her. "Speak slowly."

And so she slowed down. She said her mom and dad had been asking her about the girl from Canada who helped her when she got hurt. They wanted to meet this kind stranger and say thank you, and they had been annoyed because she hadn't thought to ask the person's name or where she was staying. The little girl peeled back the bandage on her knee and showed me the wound, so I would know it was already getting better.

"And now," she said, "you will come to my home?" She tugged on my arm again, almost falling over with the effort. She seemed totally unaware that my thoughts were somewhere else.

I looked back at Mom.

"Who is that?" asked the girl. She seemed confused, maybe because I looked Chinese and Mom didn't.

"It's my mom," I told her.

"Then she should come, too!" The girl was overexcited and yelling now. "Our mothers can be friends!"

Through the restaurant window we saw a young couple sit down at our table. They were watching us intently through the glass.

Mom said, "You clearly started something with this little girl. I think you need to go with her."

The girl pulled on my arm again. I looked back at Mom. She hadn't moved.

And the girl walked back to her and took her hand.

If she hadn't done that, would Mom have stayed right where she was? Would she have let me walk away? And what would have happened afterward? It was too frightening to think about.

But the girl took Mom's hand as if she was her own mother, and led her off. I followed maybe a step or two behind.

She told us her name was Xiao Hua. Her enthusiasm made her seem so completely different from the frightened child I'd found wailing on the sidewalk just a few days earlier. She was lively now. Very talkative. After a few steps, she leaned back to take my arm, too, as if she thought I might be planning an escape, and that's how we walked on down the sidewalk, the three of us, Xiao Hua leading, showing us where we should go.

We crossed the street, turned left and, after a short walk, Xiao Hua turned into a gray apartment building. It had the look of a place that wasn't finished yet, though lines of washing fluttered outside the windows.

In the elevator, I glanced across at Mom, but she wouldn't meet my eyes. She stared down at the worn carpet, her hands jammed into the pockets of her jeans. I wanted to know what she was thinking and if she was disappointed in me, now that things could never go back to the way they were. But from her body language, you'd think Mom was riding the elevator with her little girl, and I was only a stranger who happened to get on at the same time.

I was still holding the crumpled paper in my hand. I wanted to smooth it out and just gaze at the number. Something, finally, that connected me directly to my birth parents. But I also wanted to open my fingers and just let the paper drift to the floor. To make it go away.

There was so much new stuff to think about that my head was swimming.

My birth parents wanted to talk to me.

And my dad had another daughter.

Xiao Hua lived seven floors up. When the elevator stopped, she charged out even before the doors were fully opened, and ran ahead to let her parents know we were coming. Her mom was already waiting in the doorway when we arrived, a tiny lady with shiny skin and a nervous smile.

She stepped aside and showed us in. The apartment had almost no furniture, though in the tiny kitchen there was a scratched plastic table and several dented metal chairs. She invited us to take a seat at the table, and poured us cups of jasmine tea from a silver flask. Then Xiao Hua's father came in to introduce himself. He wore a gray business suit. Unlike Xiao Hua's mom, he spoke a bit of English. He told us that he worked nearby, at a factory that printed newspapers.

Mom didn't say a lot, not even when Xiao Hua's mother brought out a platter of sweets and dried fruits that she had likely been keeping for a special occasion. Having two Canadian visitors in their house was probably a very exciting thing for them, and we must have seemed so rude, looking all the time like we'd rather be somewhere else. Xiao Hua's parents didn't sit down with us, they hovered, trying to think of more things we might like and smiling from ear to ear the entire time.

I'd always wanted to visit with a Chinese family. Now here we were, in an actual Chinese home, being treated like long lost friends, and all I could think about was how much I wanted to be back in the hotel with time to think. Time to sort everything out inside my head.

Xiao Hua talked a lot, fast, in Chinese, filling all our silences. She brought out a doll to show me, and a beautiful book filled with paper-cuts of butterflies and flowers. Every few minutes, her mom would say something quietly, and Xiao Hua would leap into action, grabbing the sweets and offering them round, while her mom topped up our teas, even if we had drunk almost nothing at all. Xiao Hua's father spoke to us proudly in his limited English, or he used simple Chinese words so I could understand and translate for Mom.

It was a difficult conversation with a lot of gaps in it as we all figured out how to communicate, and maybe that's why a long time went by before I began to notice something strange. Mom wasn't following the conversation at all. She wasn't even trying to. She sat with her head bent, as if she was fascinated by something in her cup. But looking more closely, I realized it wasn't her tea she was staring at, it was her hand, which sat limp as a glove on the table top.

"Mom?"

She glanced up, looking puzzled, as if she was surprised to find me there. The anger had gone from her eyes, which made me relieved for a second, until I realized that what had replaced it was far worse.

Panic.

"Mom?"

Xiao Hua's father stopped talking.

When Mom spoke, her words came out slowly. Looking directly at me, she said: "I can't ... feel my hand anymore."

I didn't know what to say. I felt really scared. Mom needed my help and I didn't have the faintest clue what to do.

"Kelly, there must be a migraine coming on. A bad one. My arm feels heavy and my leg is tingling. Maybe we should leave ..."

Mom tried to stand up but she couldn't do it because she was leaning over to the left too much. By this time, even Xiao Hua could see something bad was happening. She had her doll on her knee, and she was trying to force its plastic arm into a knitted jacket. As Mom tried to get to her feet, Xiao Hua stopped what she was doing, her eyes getting wider, the doll forgotten.

"I have to go back to ..."

Mom's words trailed off to silence, as if she couldn't remember what it was she had wanted to say. Time stood still as we all stared at her. No one breathed. And that was when Mom let go of the edge of the table, which she had been gripping tightly with her good hand the entire time.

Slowly and without any fuss, which is the way she tends to do everything, Mom's body slid to the floor.

7

强大

STRENGTH

Xiao Hua's father took charge. He didn't call an ambulance; he hoisted Mom over his shoulder and hurried toward the door. For a second, I just stood there, too shocked to react—then I charged ahead of him to the elevator, slamming my hand on the *down* button again and again until the elevator came. Even before the doors had fully opened, we were inside. Seven, six, five, I counted the little lights that blinked on as the elevator moved downward. When we reached the lobby, I was the first out, running into the street, waving my arms madly, so that by the time Xiao Hua's father reached me, there was already a cab pulling over to the side of the street.

The cab crawled through crazy traffic for what seemed like forever, caught up in lanes and lanes of cars, and all the time I was screaming on the inside. I wanted the taxi driver to slam his hand on the horn and squeeze between all the other cars, his head hanging outside the window to yell at everyone to get out of his way, just like people do in movies. But that didn't happen. Mom sat in the middle of the back seat between Xiao Hua's father and me. My shoulder was supporting her head, and every few minutes she would slip a little way down my arm, like she was just a heavy backpack and not a real person at all. I had to use all of my strength to heave her upward again. It was horrible to see her there, slumped between us, mostly unconscious. One time when she slipped, I couldn't get her upright on my own, and Xiao Hua's father had to help. He hooked his hands under her armpits to pull her back to a sitting position, then his eyes caught mine. He must have realized how frightened I was because he tried to reassure me. "No sad. She ... good," he said slowly in English. But maybe she wouldn't be good. Nothing would, ever again.

All the time, throughout that endless journey, the cab driver behaved as if this was a trip like any other. He kept tuning his radio, trying to find music that he liked. I wished so badly that we had called an ambulance. I needed sirens and speed, not this endless stop and start, on and on down the highway, as if no one cared that she might die.

I cared.

Mom opened her eyes for only about a minute during our cab ride to the hospital. I wished I had used that moment to let her know how much I loved her. One more regret to add to all the others.

For months after, I had nightmares about that journey. In the nightmares, we stayed trapped on the highway while day wore into night and Mom seemed to fade away with each breath. I'd see a gap in the traffic and I'd yell and yell at the cab driver to change lanes, to get us out while he could, but no matter how much I yelled, he did nothing. In those nightmares, we never reached the hospital in time. I'd wake up sobbing, the bed sheets damp, my whole body shaking.

In reality, we were on that highway for maybe an hour.

Beijing is the busiest city I've ever been in, and the hospital we went to that day must have been in the busiest part of Beijing. The cab pulled up by the doors to the Emergency Department and, together, Xiao Hua's father and I lifted Mom out of the back seat. The waiting room was so crowded that we had to push hard on the doors, until people squeezed together enough that we could open them. Inside, every available space was crammed with patients waiting to be seen. They sat on chairs, leaned against windows, and rested on the floor. People clutched at their stomachs, nursed injured hands, or applied pressure to wounds that were bleeding. In a few places, someone injured or sick or very old lay curled up on the cold floor tiles, protected by friends or relatives who stood on guard to make sure no one stepped on them. There was a lot of pleading and shouting, drowned out occasionally by the barking of instructions over the loudspeaker system, or the wail of a siren right outside the door.

All those very sick people, and yet Mom must have been sicker than any of them, because no one made her wait in line. As soon as we arrived, an orderly fetched a gurney, spoke briefly to Xiao Hua's father and then, without even looking at me, he wheeled her away.

"Did you tell them it started with a headache?" I asked in English. I was so frightened, there was no way my brain would work in Chinese anymore. "She's always getting headaches."

Xiao Hua's father nodded. "Yes, I tell them, head hurt, and hand ..." He couldn't find the right words, so he waved his fingers in the air, then let his wrist go limp.

We stood together in a corner, jammed behind the exit door. It seemed like a lifetime that we waited. Xiao Hua's father was such a kind man. He couldn't think of anything to say that would make me feel better, but I didn't care. He stayed there beside me the whole time so I wouldn't have to be alone.

An hour later, a nurse came to find us. She spoke briefly in Chinese, then left again.

"Mom is wake," Xiao Hua's father told me. "She talk doctor. Hand work now. But they need ..." He struggled to find the words. "Make tests. Long time to wait for tests."

"Will they let me see her?"

Xiao Hua's father shook his head. He smiled apologetically. "Must wait." Then he sighed. "Kelly, sorry. I want to stay but must go, for work. There is boss. Now is late, for work. Very sorry, Kelly."

I felt scared. I didn't want to be on my own.

Xiao Hua's father pulled a cell phone from his pocket. He scrolled through several text messages, frowning.

"There is boss," he repeated, "get mad. You have money?"

"I put Mom's purse in my backpack," I said. "And she has a card with medical insurance on it."

"There is phone in bag? You have people to call? Father? Friend?"

I realized he didn't understand that Mom and I were traveling alone. He'd assumed we were part of a group, and that people were waiting for me back at our hotel. People I could turn to for help. I wished that were true.

I had nobody else except for Auntie Lou, and she was all the way back in Canada.

"It's okay," I said, because maybe if he stayed with me, he would lose his job, and that would be bad news for his whole family. I forced a smile, when really what I wanted to say was, *I'm all on my own. Please don't leave me here.*

"I have someone I can call." I told him. To prove everything would be okay, I took out Mom's cell phone and showed it to him. Xiao Hua's father glanced down at his own phone and frowned as another text message came through. I could tell he didn't want to leave me there all by myself, without any adults to take charge.

"When tests end," he told me, "there is taxi for you to take with mother." He pointed to a line of taxis just beyond the doors. "You know where is your hotel?"

I nodded. Then, with the slightest hesitation, he leaned over to hug me awkwardly and hurried off.

Leaving me alone.

For a long time, I stood in the same spot behind the exit door, clutching Mom's purse to my chest, my backpack slung over one shoulder. People around me talked to each other loudly in Mandarin, but my brain had forgotten how to understand it, and now China felt very foreign indeed. As time went on and no news came, I slid to the floor, gathering my knees up to my chest so no one would stand on me. There was a constant stream of injured people pouring into the waiting room the entire time. People clamoring, shouting, wailing, sobbing. And occasionally, someone very sick or injured, who waited mostly in silence until a gurney came to take them away. Maybe that's how they could tell if someone was seriously ill. There was no crying and fuss, just a stillness and silence.

That was exactly how it had been with Mom.

Beyond the glass exit doors, daylight faded. No pink sunset, like in Yangshuo. Just a thickening gray that turned to black. And for all those hours, the waiting room stayed busy and hectic, stuffed full of shouting, tears, and pain. It burned its way into my head until nothing else in the world existed.

Then, just when I'd started to think I'd be there all night, a doctor came to get me.

I followed him through double doors that swung closed behind us. Suddenly, the frightening noises of the waiting room were gone, and instead, dim and empty hospital corridors stretched ahead of us. The doctor walked quickly, and I almost had to run in an effort to keep up. We zigzagged right and left, took a flight of stairs, and came out in another corridor identical to all the others. Then the doctor opened the door to a room with just one bed in it. In the bed, sheets tucked all the way up to her chin, was Mom.

What I should have done was hug her and smile to help make her brave. Instead, I halted just inside the doorway and burst into tears.

The doctor looked at my mom and back at me, as if he was deciding what to do. Then he reached for a chart. He looked down at the paper as he started, in broken English, to explain.

"In brain," he said to us, "we have blood, which is ..." He halted, closing his hand into a fist. "Like this. Big ... group. Ball." He frowned.

"Clot." Mom said, her voice quivering a little. "A blood clot. I see."

"Yes, it is clot." He nodded furiously. "It is clot in brain. Very bad place, make body ..." Just like Xiao Hua's father, he raised the fingers of one hand, wiggled them, then let his hand go limp.

Mom said, "I've had a lot of tingling. Like pins and needles. Then numbness down my left side. The headaches have been getting worse, too."

The doctor frowned, as if he had no idea what she meant, but he gave several small, fast nods all the same.

"This blood clot must take out or will very bad. Very bad."

Slowly it dawned on me what it was he meant. I looked at Mom. She had figured it out, too.

"Surgery," Mom said, and she sighed. "Is there any way this can wait until we get home?"

The doctor shook his head. He did it very dramatically, swinging his head as far as it would go from one direction to the other, as if to emphasize how certain he was. "No possible. It very important to do now, for save life." He walked over to the bed and held out the chart, as if providing evidence to back up his words. Mom accepted the chart and looked at it. She probably had no clue what she was seeing. Like you'd expect, everything was in Chinese. The doctor continued, "Clot is very, very dangerous. We must take out soon. Don't wait. Tomorrow is surgeon. Our hospital very good. In week, you leave hospital."

He nodded one last time, as if to let us know this was his final decision, then he turned and left the room. I wondered whether he would have told us more, or at least given us a chance to ask questions, if we spoke fluent Chinese.

I took a tissue from beside Mom's bed and blew my nose. Then I perched on the covers beside her. The room didn't have any windows. It felt like a prison cell. Mom wasn't wearing her own clothes anymore, only a baggy hospital gown. And she had a needle sticking out of the back of her hand.

"Are you scared?" I asked.

Mom didn't answer. She was staring up at the ceiling, her forehead wrinkled with the effort of thought. It wasn't her surgery she was thinking of, though. It was me.

"Will you be able to find your way back to the hotel?" she asked. "There's plenty of money in my purse. Do you think you can find a taxi by yourself? I have a card for the Marriott, with the address in Chinese. All you have to do is show the driver the card and he'll take you there. Do you think you can do that?"

I'd done it in Yangshuo—taken a taxi alone—though Mom didn't know that, of course. So, yes, I could do it. But the thought was still kind of scary. It shouldn't be my job to deal with all this, I thought. If Dad hadn't left us, I wouldn't be facing this all by myself.

"Can't I stay here?" I asked. "With you?"

Mom shook her head. "They have a lot of rules in this hospital. They won't let you stay."

Mom must have guessed how scared I was, because her tone changed. It became firmer as she said, "You need to do this, Kelly. There's no other way. You tell me all the time that you're growing up. Well, now is your chance to show what you're capable of." I turned away from her to blow my nose again, and stared down at the floor.

"Sweetheart," Mom said softly, "we need to face the fact that I'm going to be stuck here for a while."

Her voice had a little catch in it, like she was fighting back tears.

"Don't worry," I told her. "I'll manage."

Mom said, "I want you to call Auntie Lou right away. Tell her what has happened. She'll work everything out. Can you do that?"

I thought of how Auntie Lou had visited my room on the night before we left for China, totally freaking me out. She'd given me a list of emergency numbers so I could get in touch with her, almost as if she was psychic and she knew what was going to happen. But how could she have known?

I nodded. "Her numbers are in my pocket," I said.

My mind was racing. Mom had to to have brain surgery.

What if she didn't get better? I had to fight down the panic, thinking about that.

"Mom, the thing with my birth parents ..."

She shook her head. "Not now," she said. "I can't think about that now. I just wish you'd told me. You didn't have to keep secrets."

"Neither did you."

Mom said nothing.

I climbed up onto the bed and put my head beside hers on the pillow. She didn't move for the longest time, then she reached her arm around my neck and stroked my hair, just like she used to when I was small. It felt good. So good I wanted us to stay like that forever. I thought about how scared Mom must be feeling to have surgery in a country where she didn't know anyone except me, and she couldn't even ask questions because the doctor didn't speak much English. I reached out and stroked her hair as well.

Mom sighed. "That's nice," she whispered.

Then I remembered a lullaby she used to sing to me when I was little, the two of us cuddled up together in our special rocking chair. Dad never sang me lullabies over and over until I fell asleep, but Mom used to. I felt stronger somehow, remembering that, and I wondered if Mom would remember, too, and if she did, whether the memory could help make her stronger. So I started to hum the lullaby, our special one. Mom smiled and I knew she was remembering. Then she sighed and closed her eyes. She looked so peaceful, but also very small and helpless, as if I was the adult and she was my kid. I stroked her head, she stroked my head, and we stayed like that for a really long time, just being together, until at last Mom's hand fell still on my forehead and I knew she had fallen asleep.

I waited for a while, not wanting to disturb her, then I climbed down from the bed, grabbed my backpack, and tiptoed out, easing the door shut behind me. In the corridor, I sank down against the wall and reached for Mom's cell phone. Auntie Lou's number was crumpled up in the pocket of my coat, a scrap of paper long forgotten next to another, more recent one—the phone number for my birth parents, written in Mom's untidy handwriting. I tried to imagine what might have been going through Mom's mind as she took that message for me and wrote it down.

Then I called Auntie Lou.

"Who's with you now?" she asked in her taking-charge voice, once I'd told her what had happened.

"Don't worry about me," I said, trying to sound more confident than I really felt. There was no way Auntie Lou was going to hear me cry. "Just think about Mom. I can take care of myself."

Lou said, "I need to make some calls. Give me about an hour and I'll call you back on this number. Are you sure you are all right?"

"Perfectly fine," I told her and ended the call.

I eased open Mom's door and checked inside. She was still sleeping, looking so helpless in her hospital bed that my heart fluttered with fear. But at least she was resting. There was nothing else I could do tonight.

I pocketed Lou's emergency numbers and opened up the

smaller piece of paper. Maybe it was just a line of scrawled digits, but this note was the only link I might ever have to my birth parents. It would be nice to call them. To hear my birth mom's voice. But not now. I remembered what Mom had said in the restaurant. Lots of people had walked away from me. But she never had.

If I lost my mom, nothing would be left at all.

I crumpled the piece of paper into the tiniest ball possible, then I crammed it deep down into my pocket. I thought I could feel it, solid and heavy like a lead weight, as I hurried toward the exit.

Then I waited for a taxi back to the hotel.

To: combatsleuth@mystic.com
Subject: Your Daughters

Dear Dad,
I've sent you a lot of messages in the weeks since you went away, but now for the first time I get to write one that I'm sure you'll read. Why? Because I'm using an email address I know you actually check.

It took me a long time to figure out what to say to you. I was up all last night, thinking about it. At first I poured out my feelings, trying to tell you everything I've been through since you left us. But most of that got deleted because I kept remembering that for weeks you emailed back and forth with Mom, and never once did you ask about me. Like you wanted to wipe me out of your mind as well as your life. I think maybe that gives me the right to be a bit private.

So what do I tell you? I'm in China. But then you know that already. And Mom is in the hospital. I would like to say she's going to be fine, but I can't because I don't know. Auntie Lou is coming soon, but at the moment no one is here with me. I'm all on my own. So feel free to be a bit worried about me, because you're my dad.

I met your girlfriend once. Do you remember? It was at one of your medieval festivals. We spent an afternoon together, braiding our hair and dancing. She was pretty nice to me, though not as nice as Mom, no way.

I don't think it's possible for someone to stop loving someone else after years and years, especially their daughter. So probably you miss me, even if it's not as much as I miss you. I asked Mom once if I would ever see you again, and she said I would have to wait and see. This is a phrase I hate so much—wait and see. I've been waiting and seeing for a long time now, Dad.

I'm putting my email address at the bottom here, in big letters, in case you've forgotten it. If you'd like to know about Mom and how she is doing, then you only have to ask.

You have two daughters now. Two.

Kelly

PS. In case you haven't figured it out already, I won't be coming to Vancouver any time soon.

8

家庭

FAMILY

Mom had her surgery the next morning.

I couldn't say anything to her in the last minutes before they took her away because of the huge lump stuck in my throat. I was scared that if I tried to speak, I would end up crying, and Mom didn't need that. Instead, I held onto her tightly for as long as possible. Hopefully, that said as much as words.

After they wheeled her off, I killed time by wandering through the hospital, trying hard not to think about what was being done to her. I stuck to corridors that ran along the outside walls because they had big windows, and that made me feel less trapped and panicky. Mostly I paced, but sometimes I paused to stare out over Beijing. Beyond the concrete walls of the hospital, hundreds of gray apartment blocks marched into the distance, as if that was all the world contained. A light rain was falling from a sky so heavy that it was as if the lid of a box was being lowered on us all.

After a couple of hours, I returned to Mom's room so I would be there waiting when they brought her back. I perched on the edge of her bed and watched the clock. The hands didn't seem to move at all, no matter how long I stared at them. Every time footsteps approached the room, I tensed up, hopeful, but they always walked straight on past.

Lunchtime arrived, and still there was no sign of Mom. Then a nurse came in to fetch something. She looked surprised to find me sitting on the bed all alone. I think everyone had forgotten about me. The nurse said something in Chinese that I didn't understand. I could tell she was being kind, though, because she smiled and patted my shoulder. She turned and left, returning moments later with a tiny porcelain cup of jasmine tea, which she placed in my hands.

My stomach was too churned up to drink it.

More hours went by and each one of them felt like an entire day, a week, even. It was the middle of the afternoon when the nurse came again. She beckoned to me, and I followed her down the corridor and into a different room. This one had a lot more machines in it, and several medical staff who were all too busy to notice me. There were four beds in the room, but only one of them was occupied.

The person in that bed was my mom.

When I saw her, I burst into tears, and I don't know whether I was crying with relief because she was okay, or shock because she looked so frightening. She was hooked up to a machine that kept beeping, and her face was so pale she didn't really look alive. Her bare arms looked lifeless, too, lying on top of the sheets. But the worst thing of all was Mom's hair. They had cut and shaved a whole section of it away. It hadn't occurred to me they would need to do that. Where her scalp was exposed, the skin was totally white and bumpy, like a chicken before it gets cooked. Around the edge of the shaved area, the hair had been cut roughly with scissors, leaving a lot of ragged bits. Mom also had a thick dressing that ran diagonally across one side of her head, and the edge of the dressing was red and sticky where blood had seeped through.

As I stood over her, Mom opened her eyes for a few seconds and looked at me blankly.

A doctor came in shortly after. He explained in careful English that the surgery had gone well and the clot had been removed. Mom would need to remain in hospital for at least a week to recover, he said. After that, we'd have to wait a few more days before it would be safe for her to fly home.

I sat beside Mom's bed for a long time after the doctor left, even though she seemed to have fallen into a deep sleep. It was alarming to see Mom with her hair all snipped and shaved, because usually it looked perfect. Each morning, she would stand in front of her mirror and brush it until it shone. When I was small, I'd crouch at the foot of her bed and watch her. I loved the way sunshine caught the strands as static flung them upward. Sometimes Mom was so focused on what she was doing that she would forget I was in the room. I liked the way her face looked when that happened—private and dreamy. Those mornings came to an end years ago, and I hadn't thought of them for a long time. But that was what I found myself thinking about as I sat by Mom's hospital bed.

A few hours later, Auntie Lou arrived from Toronto. She had taken a taxi straight from the airport to the hospital.

"Mom's surgery went well," I told her. "She won't have headaches anymore."

Auntie Lou approached Mom's bed. She picked up one of her limp white arms and raised it to her own cheek. It was an action filled with beauty and love, and it took me totally by surprise.

After that, we stood for a long time just looking down at Mom, but she didn't wake up. Outside the hospital, day turned into night.

"We should go back to your hotel," Lou said at last.

I led the way down the corridor and out of the hospital. We loaded Auntie Lou's bags into the back of a cab, then I spoke to our driver in Chinese, telling him the address for our hotel and agreeing what the charge would be.

"You certainly seem to have coped well by yourself," Auntie Lou said. She sounded surprised. As the cab pulled out, she kept glancing over at me, like she was seeing me for the first time. Once or twice I glanced over at her, too. I couldn't help thinking, here is someone who just flew all the way around the world because we needed her.

Then our eyes met.

We smiled at each other.

Mom spent the next ten days recovering in hospital. Visiting wasn't allowed until late afternoon, so Auntie Lou and I had a lot of time to spend with each other. For the first few days, we waited at the hotel or in the cafe at the hospital, killing time. But then, as the week wore on, Mom became stronger and there was less reason to be anxious so, between visiting hours, we started to see bits of Beijing together. I took Auntie Lou to a hutong and we visited the Summer Palace. On a different day, Auntie Lou took me to the Silk Market and I bought Mom a turquoise bag to match her Chinese jacket. And on a morning with the bluest sky I'd seen since leaving Canada, we went to Tiananmen Square.

The square wasn't anything like the plazas I'd been to in Mexico. It was a vast slab of concrete, bigger than sixty soccer fields put together, Auntie Lou said. People scurried across it like bugs, and soldiers marched around the edges with guns over their shoulders. On one wall, there was a huge portrait of a very important-looking man.

"That's Chairman Mao," Auntie Lou said.

We stared up at his enormous face together.

"In Toronto," I told her, "someone said to me that Mao made his people kill all the wild birds and eat them. But when I was in Yangshuo I saw a lot of wild birds, so I don't think that can be true."

Auntie Lou said, "Mao believed birds ate the grain in the fields. So he told everyone to kill them. Millions of birds were killed, but Mao was wrong. It was the insects that were destroying the crops. With few birds left to eat the insects, the harvest failed and a lot of people died."

We walked together into the middle of the square. I felt small, all of a sudden, and very exposed. Maybe that was why, standing right out in the middle of that vast emptiness, I told Auntie Lou everything.

I told her about Raizel and the mysterious envelope. I confessed to snooping in Mom's emails, and explained that was how I'd learned Dad hadn't really disappeared. I told her how upset I had been by Mom's lies, enough to run away, stay out all night, and go back to my birth village with Raizel's posters. And lastly, I told Auntie Lou what had happened in the restaurant. How Mom had taken the call about my birth parents and finally told me the truth: Dad had abandoned us for his girlfriend and his soon-to-be baby daughter.

Auntie Lou listened while I talked on and on. She didn't interrupt, not even once.

When I finished, neither of us spoke for a while. A little boy ran across the square, right in front of us. He was trying to fly a kite. At first the kite jumped along on the ground behind him, but then a gust of wind caught it and it rose up into the sky. I thought of another boy, on a pyramid in a yellow town far away. His kite had been no more than plastic bags tied together, yet he was so proud, it was like he was holding the world on the end of a string.

The wind fell, bringing the kite down with it, and the boy ran off.

"Why didn't my dad want to talk to me after he left?" I asked Lou. "Why do you think he didn't answer any of my emails?"

We stood together in the middle of the square and a cold wind blew round us.

"We're complicated, all of us," Auntie Lou said. "I suspect your dad was ashamed of himself. Ashamed for what he had done. He always liked to be idolized by others. Especially you. For years, he had made himself your hero. I wonder if he could cope with you seeing him for who he really was."

I pulled my spring jacket tighter around my shoulders and shivered. "What about Mom? Why didn't she tell me the truth about why Dad left? All those months, I kept thinking maybe he was sick or something, or he just needed to be alone for a while. Every day I thought, maybe this is the day my dad will come back."

Auntie Lou said, "I told your mom she might not be making the best decision, keeping things from you, but confrontation has never been easy for her. I know she was going to tell you the truth after China."

We stopped walking and Auntie Lou turned to face me. She said, "Kelly, if your mom had told you the truth about your dad, how do you think you would have reacted? What would you have done?"

I thought about how angry I'd been at Mom over the past months. It had always been easy to blame her for everything because she was the one who was right there. "If Mom had told me the truth," I said slowly, determined to be honest, "I would still have blamed her. I would have accused her of telling lies about my dad, to turn me against him."

"There you are, then."

I was surprised how wise Auntie Lou could be.

"No offense," I told her, "but when Mom said we had to move in with you, I was pretty upset. Now I don't think it would be so bad. I still don't want to move to Brantford, though. I've lost a lot of people in my life. I don't want to lose my best friend, too."

Auntie Lou produced two Snickers bars from her bag. She handed one of them to me. We watched the soldiers as they marched past.

"Nothing's finalized yet," Lou said.

"I miss Raizel a lot. Did you know there isn't even Facebook in China? Sometimes I just want to talk to her."

I thought Auntie Lou would brush this off as silly, but she didn't. "Nowadays," she said, "most of us live a long way from our families. Friends can be as important as family to your generation."

We took a bite of our candy bars, both at the same time.

"I have my laptop at the hotel," she added. "If you want, you can use it to Skype with your friend."

We walked across the square and back toward the subway, and I was thinking about what a kind offer that was, and how many things I had to tell Raizel, when out of the blue I remembered something. I stumbled, grabbing hold of Auntie Lou.

"Oh, no!"

"Kelly? What's wrong?"

"I sent Mom an email," I gasped, "that day in Yangshuo when I found all the messages from Dad! I was angry at her. I didn't stop to think. The message said, 'WHY DID YOU

KEEP MY DAD FROM ME?' Auntie Lou, Mom hasn't checked her emails yet but when she does, she'll read it!" I breathed deeply a few times, trying to calm down. "I want us both to be able to start over, I really do, but when Mom reads that message and realizes I went through her emails, she's going to get mad at me all over again."

Auntie Lou said, "I suspect your mom has figured out you read her emails, Kelly."

I thought about this. She must have her suspicions. It was the only way I could have known for sure that she was keeping Dad from me. But Mom probably wanted a fresh start for us both as much as I did.

Auntie Lou looked thoughtful for a minute, then she smiled.

"Reading someone else's personal messages is wrong," she said. "I think you know that. But under the circumstances, you may be doing both of you a favor if you access your Mom's emails just one more time."

With Mom in hospital for so long, I had a lot of time on my hands. Every morning I checked my email on Auntie Lou's laptop, hoping that Dad might get in touch. For the first few days there was nothing, and that hurt me so much that each time it felt like losing him all over again. But then, an entire week after my email message to him, I got this:

To: kellybelly@sherwoodproductions.ca
Subject: [blank]

Kelly,
How is your mom doing?
Dad

The email didn't ask how I was. It didn't tell me anything about Dad's new life, and it didn't explain why he had left us. There wasn't even a "Love, Dad" at the end. Getting a message like that felt almost worse than no message at all.

"Why, Dad?" I said out loud.

Why?

Maybe the message was short because Dad felt guilty, like Auntie Lou had said. He didn't think he had the right to get back in touch after everything he had done. Maybe he needed to know he was forgiven first.

Well, that was dumb. I didn't forgive him and maybe I never would. My dad had walked out on me. He left me even though he knew that I'd already been abandoned once. To have that happen all over again, how did he think that would feel? It was too much to forgive.

"You wrecked everything," I told his email. "You were selfish and stupid and you wrecked everything."

I couldn't imagine a time when I'd stop being angry at Dad.

But that didn't mean I wanted him out of my life forever. He was still my dad, and maybe I wasn't as good at abandoning people as he was. Somehow, that thought made me feel very good about myself.

I hit *reply*.

Dad (I wrote)

Mom will be out of the hospital soon. Auntie Lou came to be with me. You were wrong about her. She's a good person, and she's helping us both. We are mostly doing fine and I hope you are, too.

Kelly

On Mom's last day in hospital, I got invited to Xiao Hua's school as a guest.

This visit was very different from the first one. Xiao Hua took me by the hand and led me into her classroom, smiling proudly. All the children clapped when we entered and chanted: "Good morning, visitor, and how do you do?" In that moment, standing there in front of them all, I felt like the Queen of England.

Xiao Hua's teacher asked me to help the children with their English, so we turned the classroom into a restaurant and all the kids got to be customers, ordering their meals. I played the server, weaving between the little desks with my notepad. "What would you like to eat for dinner?" I asked each of them, keeping a very straight face. The children giggled and tried to think of English words like noodles, rice, and chicken. One little boy laughed so hard, he slid under his desk, and the teacher had to stop the role play and get her classroom back under control. But later she said I was so good with all the children that maybe, once I was done school, I should come back and teach English in China. I had no idea people did things like that.

As the lesson came to an end, all the kids moved up to the

front of the class, standing in neat rows, and sang a traditional song just for me, while I sat crammed behind one of the desks, my knees up to my chin, proud and unbelievably happy. I thanked each one of them in English and in Chinese. Then I wrote down the school's address and promised to send candy made of maple syrup once we got home. As I was about to leave, one of the boys grabbed my arm and shouted: "Toronto Blue Jays!" So I guess they know a bit about Canada after all.

During the lunch recess, Xiao Hua gave me a tour of her school, holding my hand tightly and marching me up and down the halls. In the last room we came to, right at the top of the building, there were rows and rows of little beds, all with bedding neatly rolled up at the bottom and pajamas folded on the pillows. So some of these little children stayed at school all week. I wondered how it would feel to be five or six years old and not see your mom and dad for days at a time. Life isn't always perfect, even for kids who have their birth parents.

That afternoon, we went to the hospital to pick up Mom.

"You can have your own hotel room now, if you like," Auntie Lou said as we left the hospital parking lot by taxi for the last time. "I don't mind sharing with your mom."

But I didn't want that. Mom and I were a family. Maybe a small one now, but still a family. It was up to the two of us to take care of each other.

Back at the hotel, I unlocked our room and heaved Mom's suitcase inside. I turned to see Mom pause in the doorway, a defeated expression on her face. I followed her gaze. On the wall behind me was a full-length mirror. Mom was staring at her ruined hair.

"Frankenstein's monster," she said.

"It's going to grow back," I told her. Mom turned away and started to unpack. But later, she draped a bathrobe over the mirror so she wouldn't have to look at herself.

While Mom took a shower, I Skyped with Raizel. I told her how good it felt to finally have my mom out of the hospital.

"You must be relieved," Raizel said. "Brain surgery is major, you know that? She could have died!"

I changed the subject.

"You know our graphic novel?" I asked. "Well, I have this really cool art thing for us to try when I get back. It's a Chinese way of painting, where you only use ink and the side of your hand. I can't wait to show you."

"Cool," Raizel said. "We still have to finish working on the plot, though. I think we should make Vasa an orphan." It felt good, hearing my best friend talk about normal stuff we did together. In only a few days I would be home. China and all of this would be a world away.

"Vasa's parents aren't dead," I told her. "She only thinks they are. The Painted People have them. There's a quest and Vasa saves both their lives."

Raizel leapt out of her seat with a squeal. For a moment, all I could see was a blur as she ran around her room. "That's so cool!" she yelled. "I love, love, love, love, love it!" There was a pause and her face loomed large on the screen again. Suddenly, Raizel looked very serious. "Did you put my posters up, Kelly?" she asked. "I need to know. Did you go looking for your birth mom and dad?"

I wasn't ready to answer that question. It's okay to be a bit private, sometimes.

Later that afternoon I was down in the gift store, trying to find a thank you present for Xiao Hua's dad, when a luxury coach pulled up outside. Within seconds, a ton of people piled into the lobby, chatting loudly. I turned around, planning to head back to our room.

Standing behind me, waiting for me to notice her, was Clare.

And in her arms was a baby.

I recognized the baby right away from her referral photos. Thick, glossy black hair. Eyes wide and alert. Clare was wearing the baby in a sling across her chest, so her thin little legs dangled freely. One of the baby's arms had escaped from the top of the sling and was reaching up, grabbing at her mom's earring.

"Clare!" I cried. "I didn't think I'd see you again!"

Clare held out one of her daughter's little hands. "Meet Phoenix," she said proudly. "Phoenix Michaela. The middle name is for her dad, Michael."

I watched the baby wriggle a bit, her hand reaching again and again for the earring, and ending up instead with a twist of her mother's hair.

"Was she ... is she ..."

"She's been very ill," Clare said. "She had pneumonia, and probably also an allergic reaction to the antibiotics they gave her. And she's lactose intolerant, I think, which has also affected her health. It's been a tough few days, but nothing we can't handle together." Clare stroked her daughter's head. I smiled at the baby and she grinned back. She only had two teeth so her smile was cute and funny at the same time.

"It was very frightening," Clare said, "but really, there was only one possible choice. Phoenix is my daughter." She glanced down at the suitcases around her feet. "Maybe we could join you and your mother for dinner one night," she said, "if you're in Beijing long enough ..."

That's when I had a brainwave.

"Clare," I said, "if you have any time free tomorrow, do you think you could do something for my mom?"

Clare did wonders with Mom's hair, shaping and styling it so the bald parts didn't show. As she worked, Mom watched in the mirror, her confidence returning. Now she looked like her true self again. As the two mothers chatted, I crouched down on the carpet and played with baby Phoenix. She had been sick for a long time, and she was having to relearn how to do a lot of things such as clapping her hands, feeding herself finger foods, and even sitting up by herself. She wasn't quite strong enough yet to pull herself up off the carpet and into a sitting position. Again and again she toppled sideways, but I always managed to catch her, so there were no tears, only giggles, as if the whole thing was just a game.

"I'm old enough to babysit, you know," I said, glancing up at Clare. She was running a comb gently around the area where Mom's stitches had been. "If you ever need a night off, I can take care of Phoenix."

Clare smiled. It was still the sad/happy smile, but now there was a lot more happy in it. "When I need a babysitter," she said, "I'll be sure to call you first. But right now, I can't imagine leaving her, not even for a second." Oh well, I thought. Mom was moving us both to Brantford, anyway. Not only far from Raizel and all my school friends. Far from Clare and Phoenix, as well.

Two days before the flight home, Mom, Auntie Lou, and I took a trip to the Great Wall.

Spring had finally come to that part of China. All the trees were in bud, and some had tiny pink blossoms starting to open. We took a bus from Beijing, then climbed a steep flight of stone steps that led up onto the wall. Lou and I took it easy for Mom's sake, but she seemed to do just fine. We stood for a long time next to one of the guard towers, enjoying the view. A patchwork of golden fields, tiny houses, rolling hills.

"I feel like going for a bit of a hike," Lou said, "if you two can cope without me. See you back at the bus in an hour?" Her cheeks were flushed and she seemed happy all of a sudden. I wondered how long it was since she had been on a holiday. She didn't seem the type to take time for herself. We watched her stride out along the wall, a jaunty figure in a brown woolen skirt and leather boots.

Mom turned to me. "Sweetheart," she said, "there are some things you need to know."

Then she tried to explain about Dad. She told me she had known, almost right away, why he had left and where he was going. She had emailed him, not to ask him to come back because she knew he wouldn't. Just about practical things. And they had spoken, on and off, in the months that followed. "At first I just couldn't figure out a way to tell you," Mom said, "and then after a while, it seemed too cruel. I wasn't sure you would cope with knowing the truth, when you were already struggling with so much." Mom rubbed absently at the spiky patch on her head where new hair was already growing in. "I could have encouraged your dad to contact you," she said, "but I didn't. Until he was ready to be a proper father again, I thought it was better if he wasn't in your life at all."

I didn't know what to say. It hadn't been better. Thinking Dad had totally forgotten me was the worst thing ever. But it didn't seem right to tell Mom this, not now. I shoved my hands deep into the pockets of my coat, wondering what to say to her. And my fingers closed around a tiny ball of paper.

I took it out and peeled it open while Mom watched. On it, written in a hasty scrawl, was a phone number. We stared at it together, Dad's emails suddenly forgotten.

"I was going to throw it away," I told her.

Mom looked at me. "You shouldn't do that," she said.

I shrugged. "But I don't want to call them. Not anymore. I don't know why."

Mom took my hand in hers.

"Maybe you can't imagine getting in touch with them now, but perhaps next year, or the year after ..."

I slid the little piece of paper from the palm of my hand and into Mom's.

"Keep it for me," I said.

Mom smoothed it out and slipped it into the back of her purse. Then she held her purse out to me, so I could see exactly where it was.

"Until you need it," she said and she opened her arms.

We held onto each other for a really long time. Below us, tour buses emptied. There was an old woman selling postcards to the tourists. A man with a camera and tripod, taking photos. And next to a line of yellow cabs, a little cafe with plastic tables, blue chairs, and umbrellas open against the sun as if it was the middle of summer.

"Let's go get ourselves a nice cup of jasmine tea," Mom said, and we slowly walked down together.

At long last, Mom was well enough for us all to go home. Our bags were packed and, in just an hour, we would be off to the airport. A twelve-hour direct flight back to Toronto. No layover in Vancouver.

Home.

But there was one last thing that I needed to do.

I headed out of our hotel and walked to the end of the road, to the small park where the Tai Chi people met. I stood for a long time and watched the looping pattern of their moves—strong, graceful, and full of purpose. Like the movement of wild birds across the river near Yangshuo.

I cleared my mind of all its thoughts and matched my breathing to their rhythm. Cars hooted, sirens blared, and a city of twenty million people surged around me, but I lost sense of it all.

I stepped smoothly and proudly into line. My body found the pattern, a pattern that was hundreds of years old, and began to work through it. There was music in the moves and it pulsed inside me, right to the center of who I was, pulling me back into myself, and into a place where I would always belong.

Beginnings

We moved house that summer. Not away from Toronto, which neither of us really wanted in the end, but to a bright apartment above a bakery, one street over from Raizel's. We chose the apartment together and, with help from Cara and Raizel, we painted the most fantastic murals all over the walls. Each morning, I woke to the smell of baking: cheese bread, blueberry bagels, raisin loaves, chocolate croissants.

I started doing Tai Chi again—not because it reminded me of Dad, but because every time I worked through the moves, it brought back memories of China. It was difficult to find a place to practice, though, until one Saturday, I took a shortcut through High Park on my way to the subway, and heard traditional Chinese music somewhere in the distance. I stopped between two willows and let my body fall into the moves it knew so well. I was kind of in a trance for a bit and, when I came out of it, I saw that a Chinese couple had joined in behind me. After that, we met most weekends, and others soon joined in. There are ten of us now. Sometimes people stop to watch us, but we don't care.

Mom and I get to see Clare and little Phoenix practically every week because they only live a few streets away. We helped celebrate Phoenix's first birthday, and we were right beside her when she took her first steps. Sometimes I talk to her in Chinese so she won't forget how it sounds. And when she's older, I'll be there for her if she ever feels alone or confused about who she is.

A few days ago, Clare gave me a gift. It's a little red album with photos of the orphanage where Phoenix and I both spent the first few months of our lives. Clare was the only one of us who got to visit, in the end.

Dad emailed me on and off through spring and into summer, but his emails were always short, and more like something you'd write to a stranger than to your own daughter. Then one day in early August, I was hanging out at Raizel's. We were finishing the storyboard for our graphic novel. It had a name now: *The Quest for the Druid's Sword.* We were mostly chatting, proud to have it all planned out, when my new cell phone rang.

"Yup?"

"Kelly ... it's me. It's your dad."

All the anger and hurt came flooding back, and there was a part of me that just wanted to throw the phone at the wall. But what I felt most when I heard his voice that day was hope. I hadn't forgiven him—maybe I would never completely forgive him—but I still wanted to hold him there on the phone. I was terrified that if I said the wrong thing, he'd slip away again.

"I called your mom," Dad said, "and she gave me this number. How are you?"

"Okay, Dad."

Raizel was sitting beside me on her bed and she just about exploded from shock. She kept giving me signals, and trying to tell me what to say, but this was about me and my dad and no one else. I walked into the bathroom and locked the door.

"How is your mom?"

"Great. No more headaches."

"That's good. I'm pleased to hear it."

A pause. "And how are you?"

He was asking at last.

"I'm doing better, Dad."

There was an awkward silence after that. I tried to think of something, anything, to say, but my mind was a blank. Dad filled the silence in the end.

"I'm flying to Ontario next week," he said. "I've a jousting gig at the Scottish Festival in Fergus. I'd like to see you. If that's what you want."

My heart skipped a beat. I wanted to yell, Yes! Of course it's what I want!

But I didn't. I took a deep breath and thought it through. I still loved my dad deep down, but he couldn't expect to walk away from me and then, after all this time, put everything back the way it was in the space of one phone call.

Dad suggested a few places for us to meet, and they were all spots that had been special to us when I was small. Places that would make me feel emotional—a kid on a day out with her dad, like everything was just fine. I said no. Those days were gone. Not Leslie Street Spit. Nowhere like that. We needed to meet in a place that wasn't loaded with memories.

Then I knew exactly where it should be.

The next Saturday, as we worked through our Tai Chi moves in High Park, we had an audience. I could tell he was there, standing under one of the willows, watching me. For the longest time I didn't look at him. I worked through the moves, one after the other, following the pattern I knew so well. Dad was scared. I knew that. A part of him wanted to just walk away. And I was so scared to lose him that I felt like running into his arms before he could disappear.

Except I didn't. On my terms, I told myself. It was a phrase I'd learned from Auntie Lou when I told her about Dad's call.

I was the one who got to decide things now. If Dad came back into my life, even a little bit, then it should be on my terms.

So we ran through the moves, again and again, while Dad watched from under the willow, trying to pluck up enough courage to do something. He had to want it enough. It wasn't going to work between us unless he wanted it enough.

After about half an hour of this, an endless half hour, I looked up.

Above us all, high in a tree, was a red-tailed hawk.

Dad must have seen it. Of course he had. I kept my eye on the hawk, my body on automatic now, working through the moves it knew so well.

And when I looked back down, Dad was right there, beside me. Not on the sidelines anymore, but in the midst of everything, matching his moves to mine.

Afterward, we went to the restaurant in the middle of the park and ate fries on the patio. I asked about my baby half-sister, and Dad opened his wallet to show me her picture. He didn't have just one photo in his wallet, he had two. One was a photo of a cute little baby with wispy tufts of red hair. The second was a not-so-recent photograph of his first daughter. Me.

One question Dad asked me while we ate was how Mom and I were coping on our own. I didn't answer him on that one, because maybe he gave up the right to know how we were doing the day he walked out on us. But the truth is, we're doing just fine. More than fine, in fact, and better every day. Turns out travel is a passion we both share, though neither of us realized it before. Sometimes we read travel books together, figuring out all the places we're going to visit when the next school holidays come around.

We often talk about doing a longer trip back to China, and we're saving hard to make it happen. Sometimes Mom says, "We could look up your birth parents the next time we go, if you like."

One day I'll do it for sure, but it has to be the right time. I figure I'll know when that time comes. So whenever Mom mentions this, I just shrug and give her a small sad-happy smile.

"I don't know, Mom," I say. "Why don't we just wait and see?

Acknowledgments

I would like to thank the faculty and students in the Optional-Residency MFA Program in Creative Writing at the University of British Columbia, especially Gail Anderson-Dargatz, Maggie De Vries, and Nancy Lee, for everything they taught me about the writing and editing process; Nikki Linton and Janet Hepburn for reading the manuscript prior to submission; Stuart Ross for his invaluable writing advice; Stephen Charles, who told me more than twenty years ago that I needed to live in a house filled with books; Wendy Ni and Maddie Wen Cao for advising on the Pinyin translations, and Peter Carver for being the best editor I could have wished for.

Huge thanks to all the wonderful girls (and boys) of the Chinese adoption community here in Ontario who inspired me to write this story, and to the staff and campers at Centauri Summer Arts Camp, whose creativity and boundless energy each summer never fail to springboard me into a year of enthusiastic writing. Enormous thanks to my incredible family and friends, who have always accepted my eccentricities with good humor. Most of all, boundless and heartfelt thanks to Craig—the absolute opposite of the father in my novel—who has always supported my dreams and who never once stopped believing in me.

Interview with Julie Hartley

What led you to write this story?

The idea for *The Finding Place* first came to me when I was standing on a pyramid in Mexico watching a boy fly a homemade kite, just as Kelly does in my novel. I remember thinking that the boy likely had Mayan ancestry, and that even if he found this part of himself intriguing, it might be difficult for him to fully understand and connect with it.

It occurred to me that this is true of all of us, in a way. We are all of us filled with secrets: stories, ancestors, cultural histories that make up who we are. I'm originally from Northeast England, and one of my family members has a disease that affects his fingers—the disease was brought over to England by the Vikings over a thousand years ago, so people who contract it have solid proof they are descended from Vikings! What does that mean, though? There's no way they can ever truly connect with that Viking part of who they are.

Our own family was formed through international adoption, just like Kelly's. Children who are adopted often have limited knowledge of their birth parents and personal history, and in the case of adoption from China, usually no knowledge at all. For international adoptees, even their heritage can be a mystery, because they are being raised in an environment very different from that of their birth parents.

But this is true of all of us, to a lesser or greater degree. The world is a very different place today than it was only a generation ago, so we all have parts of our histories, our family stories, that will never be completely knowable. We are all a mystery to ourselves. That's a perplexing thought, for sure. But it can also be something magical. This idea intrigued me, and I think it was what inspired me to start writing *The Finding Place.*

In part, the story is about a young person's search for who she really is. Why do you think this is especially important / difficult for an adopted child?

Our sense of who we are often comes from our parents, our family, and our culture. For children who are adopted, it can feel like there is a piece of the puzzle missing. In today's world, though, I think this is a perspective a lot of young people can identify with. Many children are raised away from the culture they were born into, or the culture their parents were born into, because families move around so much, and our world is so global. As we move towards adulthood, I think all of us have unanswered questions about who we are and where we come from.

It's important to remember, too, that for Kelly, being adopted isn't what triggers all the questions about identity. Her struggles begin when her father leaves the family without explanation. Families fragment all the time, and when that happens everyone involved is left feeling a little adrift—not just the children but the adults, too. The people who surround us help define who we are; they give us our place in the world. Whenever our family structure changes, our sense of self undergoes a seismic shift. It's this kind of shift Kelly is struggling with at the beginning of the novel. But the fact that Kelly knows so little about her birth culture, and next to nothing about her birth family, certainly complicates things as she struggles to redefine herself.

Kelly is a nervy, outspoken girl. In what ways do these aspects of her character help her get through the difficulties she faces?

We all have our defenses. Kelly hides behind anger a lot of the time. This offers her protection, for sure, but it also damages the relationship she has with her mother. Kelly says and does things all the time that she is likely to regret. An important part of growing up is figuring out the defenses we have at our disposal, and learning to use them properly. By the end of the novel, Kelly is able to hold her anger in check a little more, and to think before acting. Being nervy and outspoken certainly helps Kelly overcome her difficulties, but at times, it also makes things worse!

What was the most difficult challenge for you in writing this story?

I wrote the first draft of the novel in a very short time—just over a week, in fact! *The Finding Place* was written in Mexico, and I worked on it for about seven hours a day, filling page after page with hasty scrawl I could barely read, and living inside Kelly's world. So that wasn't hard at all; in fact, it was wonderful, all-consuming, and the best way I can think of to write a novel. Editing was more of a challenge, and took a lot more time! Part of a writer's job is being willing to strike scenes that don't serve the story well, even if you feel personally attached to them. I always find this difficult. Some of the chapters in my first draft were completely rewritten, whole segments were removed, and new chapters were added as I worked on later drafts.

Research must have been really important as you created Kelly's story. What did you have to do in the way of finding out about your main character?

I wanted to show how Kelly learns to connect with the magical part of her heritage through the people and scenery she encounters in China, and for that I had to travel! I explored hutongs in Beijing, and toured a school very similar to the one Kelly visits. I traveled by overnight train through China all the way to Guilin. I wanted to see the Karst formations for myself, and walk along the Li River. I based the Li River Inn on a little lodge we stayed in, just outside Yangshuo. We also took a bamboo raft down the river, and watched fishermen catch fish using cormorants. I tried to see everything through Kelly's eyes.

Your own family was formed by international adoption. In what ways was your real life journey different from that of the Stroud family?

Kelly and her story are entirely fictional. This was important to me. However, being a part of the international adoption community, and knowing so many people whose families were formed through adoption, I did feel qualified to tell Kelly's story accurately.

The circumstances of her adoption are not unusual. At the time of our first trip to China, there were tens of thousands of babies needing homes, and for most of them, their only chance at a family was through international adoption. The babies were usually left by their birth families outside public buildings such as hospitals or schools, because in China it was illegal to give up a baby, even if you had no way to take care of the child. Efforts were always made by the authorities to locate the parents and to place these children in Chinese homes if at all possible, so most of the babies were at least nine months old by the time they were adopted by families from other countries.

Generally, the babies were in good health, but occasionally a parent would be faced with a difficult decision, just as Clare was in my novel. The story of Phoenix is fictional, but similar things happened to many families. After a baby is referred to their new family overseas, usually about eight weeks elapse before the parents can travel to China. That's enough time for the baby to contract a disease, or even to be diagnosed with a health problem that may have long term implications. If this happened, the new parents might face a very difficult decision.

The international adoption scene is changing now. Tens of thousands of children were adopted out of China into families in North America and Europe over a period of about twelve years, most of them into loving homes they would never otherwise have had. Recently, China relaxed its one-child policy and a lot more has been done to encourage domestic adoption. This means there are no longer as many babies in such desperate need of a home, which of course is fantastic.

What written accounts did you find that provided insights into Kelly's search for her finding place?

I followed a lot of blogs, in the years when we were waiting to become parents. Many of those blogs charted the journey of other couples adopting from China. I also read a lot of books about life in China, while I was working on my novel. One I would love to recommend is *The Diary of Ma Yan: The Struggles and Hopes of a Chinese Schoolgirl.*

There are very few books for young people, though, with a Chinese adoptee as the protagonist. This was another reason I wanted to write *The Finding Place.* I think it's important for all of us to see ourselves reflected in the books that we read. Kelly is a regular thirteen-year-old trying to grow up. She is also an urban, North American teen who must deal with the breakup of her family. And she's an international adoptee. She is all of those things.

This is your first novel for teenagers. What would be your advice to young people interested in embarking on their own writing project?

First of all, write about what matters to you. If you feel connected to your story, it will pull you in and the writing will be pleasurable. If writing is something you love to do, then you are a writer, plain and simple. Many of my creative writing students say they only feel truly happy when they have a writing project on the go. If that describes you, then just do it! Find a little time in every day, no matter how busy you are, even if it's just five minutes.

Writing has to be something you love. This comes first. Then, if you want to get better at it, consider that writing is also a craft. Learn how to do it well, by sharing your work with people whose opinions you value. When you write something, no matter how proud you are of it, see it as the start of a process, and always ask yourself how you can make it better. There are many writing camps and classes out there these days, and many resources online, so there are plenty of opportunities for young writers to learn the craft. It's also important to connect with other young people who love writing, so you know you are not alone.

When you create a story, you carry a world inside your head that is yours and yours alone until you are ready to share it. That's why writing is so enriching, so appealing. Your story becomes a part of who you are. Writing is hard work, and the craft part of it is challenging, for sure. But when you write, you create worlds that didn't exist before, and fill them with characters and stories that spring to life only because your fingers move across a keyboard, or your pen makes marks on paper. It's hard to think of anything more magical than that.

Thank you, Julie.